BRAZEN BIKER

JESSICA AMES

COCKY HERO CLUB WORLD

Brazen Biker is a standalone story inspired by Vi Keeland and Penelope Ward's *Cocky Bastard*. It's published as part of the Cocky Hero Club world, a series of original works, written by various authors, and inspired by Keeland and Ward's *New York Times* bestselling series.

To Kerry. Thank you for believing in this story.

ONE

CARLA

HE'S SITTING at the end of the bar when I come back from my break. There's no denying the man is built. Even from here, I can see he has thick muscular tattooed arms that strain beneath the white tee he's wearing and dark hair that is pulled into a tie at the nape of his neck. It makes him look wild, like he can't be tamed. There's a layer of scruff on his jaw that's in danger of moving from a five o'clock shadow into beard territory, and beneath all that hair is a dimple. Not two, but just one, on his left side. Somehow, that makes it hotter.

He's also staring right at me, grinning like I'm the best thing he's ever seen.

When he holds his empty glass up and shakes it, internally, I groan. I know this guy's type—cocksure and an asshole to boot—but he's sitting in my section of the bar, meaning I need to serve him.

With a sigh, I move over to him, grabbing a cloth as I go. I wipe the counter in front of him, just to keep my hands busy, so I don't slap that smug smile off his damned face. I'm pretty sure my boss might kill me if I get into it with another patron.

"What can I get you?" My voice is level, bored even, giving no indication the smile is working, even if it is stirring something in my belly.

"Are you on the menu, darlin'?" His accent is thick, broad, and he's clearly not native to Temecula. The drawl of his words tells me he's a New Jersey boy. I grew up there myself, only moving out to California in my early twenties. I wanted to put as much distance as I could between me and my family. I love my dad, but his lifestyle isn't one I agree with.

I roll my eyes at his eyebrows waggling, resisting the urge to groan. Working in a bar, and looking the way I do, I get hit on a lot. My raven black hair is styled in vintage old school curls, like a nineteen forties pin up, and my arms are a colorful array of tattoos. I wear blood red lipstick and while I don't go overboard with the rest of my makeup, it's clear I'm wearing it. I'm used to cheesy pickup lines, but I didn't think he'd be the type to deliver them. He looks like the kind of man you don't take home to meet your parents, not a regular Casanova.

I arch a brow at him and this makes his dimple stand out even more, which has my stomach doing somersaults. I keep my expression neutral even so. "Does that line usually work?"

"I don't know. It's the first time I've tried it." He peers up at me, interlacing his fingers on the bar top. "Did it?"

I stare at him. "What can I get you?" I repeat my earlier question, hoping this asshole might get a clue.

"How about a date? You, me, on a one-way trip."

"I don't date."

"What? Ever? What a sad little life that must be."

"I don't date cocky assholes who hit on me at work," I correct.

He was right the first time. I don't date at all. The last guy I hit on, I followed him back to his motel and took all my clothes off, offering myself completely to him, only to be turned down. I'm a strong woman, but the rebuttal still stung like a bitch, even now, but I don't have any hard feelings toward Chance. He was crazy over his woman, Aubrey, and I was never in with a shot.

"What about when you're off the clock?"

I sigh, rubbing at my head. This guy is persistent. "Do you want a drink or not?"

"Put another Scotch in there, Carla."

I freeze mid-reach for the glass, my creep alert going haywire. Slowly, I straighten my spine and I narrow my gaze at him, giving him my best glare. "How do you know my name?"

He grins back at me. "Retract the claws, Kitten. Your dad told me it." He pulls something from his back pocket and slides it onto the counter. "Even gave me a picture of you. I've got to say, sweetheart, it doesn't do you justice."

I peer down at the photograph on the bar and see it's one of me just before I left home six years ago. I'm younger and my hair is loose, falling straight down my back. I hadn't discovered my love of vintage yet. I'm sitting outside the Savage Riders' clubhouse, though I don't remember the picture being taken.

I snatch it off the bar and he reaches for it at the same time. I'm faster and I clutch it to my chest like it's a live bomb.

"Where did you get this?" I hiss at him.

"Told you… your dad. Gunner gave it to me, so I'd be able to recognize you."

I flinch at the mention of my dad's road name. It's been a long time since I've heard it used. Too long since I'd last been in New Jersey, involved in that life, and that's how I liked it.

"My dad sent you?" He nods. "Why?"

"To bring you home."

I must have misheard because there's no way in hell I'm going back to Jersey, and my father knows it. We talk often on the phone and he's come out to Temecula over the years, but I haven't been home in a long time, and I have no plans to go back either.

"No."

"Not up for discussion, sweetheart. I was sent by Prez to bring you home, and I'm bringing you home, even if I have to tie you to the back of my bike."

He looks like the prospect of this absolutely thrills him. Anger burns a path through my gut at his words.

"I'm not a member of your club. You don't get to boss me around."

"I'm not going back without you."

I drop a hand to my hip and glare at him, shooting fire from my eyes. "Why do I need to go back?"

He rubs a hand over his jaw, his eyes serious. "Some shit's going down at the club. Your pops wants to know you're safe."

My stomach lurches at his words, fear climbing up my spine. I know things happen, but hearing about it first-hand scares me. "What kind of stuff? Is Dad okay?"

"It's club business," which means keep my nose out of it, "but it could be bad."

All signs of his grin have disappeared and he looks as serious as his words. Ice fills my belly. What the hell is my father into now?

"What's your name?"

"Rooster."

I blink and then narrow my eyes. "Your name is Rooster?" He's definitely a biker with a name like that. They all have crazy monikers. My dad's real name is Robert, but everyone calls him Gunner. I don't remember the last time I heard his real name spoken.

He smirks. "Said so, didn't I?"

"Where's your cut?" He's not wearing the leather vest all bikers wear—their club colors. I've never known a brother get on a bike without them, so it's strange to see him sitting there in just jeans and a leather jacket over the top. It makes me suspicious. Just because he knows things about me, doesn't mean he's who he says he is.

"Didn't think it was a good idea to announce to the world who I am, all things considered."

That statement sends chills racing through me. It means the club itself is a target, which is probably why my father wants me back. Out here, in California, I'm thousands of miles from home and the protection of the Savage Riders. I'm easy pickings.

"What's going on?"

"I told you—it's club business—but for your own safety we need to leave. Now."

"Well, *Rooster*, I can't just leave. I have a job."

"Your job ain't important. The club'll take care of you, but we need to go."

"No."

"Your pop said you might put up a fight." His grin returns. "I was hoping you would. You'd look so good tied to the back of my bike."

I scowl at him. "You touch me and I'll cut your fingers off."

"Come on, sweetheart, don't make this harder than it has to be."

"I'm calling my father," I mutter, pulling my cell from my apron pocket.

Rooster sits back at the bar, still looking smug as hell as I dial.

Dad answers on the second ring, his gruff voice temporarily a balm to my soul, until I remember I'm pissed at him for sending this Rooster asshole to me. *"Sweetheart, I know what you're going to say—"*

"You don't have the first clue what I'm about to say," I fire back, fury making my words sharp. "What the hell is going on?"

"You need to go with Rooster. Please, darlin'. Shit is hot back home and I need to know you're safe."

"Hot how, and if you say 'club business' I'm going to scream."

He lets out a breath. *"Come home, Carla, and I'll explain everything, I promise."*

"If I leave I'm going to lose my job." I probably won't, but I'm feeling dramatic.

"Better than your life." When I draw in a sharp breath, he adds, *"Don't want to scare you, darlin', but that's the reality we're facing here. Do as Rooster says, yeah? I trust that crazy fucker with my life."*

I grit my teeth. I want to argue with him, but growing up in the Savage Riders, I know when the club is telling me to hunker down, I better hunker down—even if I don't like it.

"Fine," I grind out. "I'll see you in a few days."

I hang up and pocket my cell. Rooster is staring at me like the cat who got the cream.

"Ready to leave?" he asks.

"I have to tell my boss I'm going. I can't just walk out."

He gestures with his hand, as if to say by all means.

Asshole.

I make up some excuse about a family emergency to my boss, Tim, and get the hell out of there before any more questions can be asked.

When we step outside the bar, the air is warm, even

despite the late hour. I come to a stop when I see a Harley parked up at the curbside.

"You brought your bike?"

He shrugs. "Don't do cages."

By cages he means cars, but seriously, is he expecting me to ride nearly three thousand miles behind him? He's crazy if he thinks that's going to happen.

"I'm not riding bitch behind you, Rooster."

His shoulders shift again in that infuriating way. "Ride bitch or walk—those are the choices."

I stare at the bike, taking in the beauty of the chrome pipes and the artwork covering the tank. It is a stunning piece of machinery and in my younger years, I wanted nothing more than to be able to ride with the boys. I realized quickly that wasn't going to be an option, that because I was a girl I would never be able to get my cut. That drove me crazy for a long time. As I got older, I realized the dangers that came from being in a one percent motorcycle club and I came to understand that life wasn't one I wanted. I'd seen my share of brothers die or disappear into the penal system. I didn't want to be looking over my shoulder, expecting the cops to turn up at any time, or wondering when I might get a phone call saying my dad was dead. I didn't want any of it, and I sure as hell didn't want a biker in my life romantically, which makes Rooster's flirting annoying. He might be attractive as all hell, but he doesn't have a chance.

"I'll walk."

He cocks his head and stares at me a beat before he asks, "Are you always so difficult?"

"Only with bikers," I mutter.

"This ain't ideal, sweetheart, but it is what it is." He hands me one of the helmets that is attached to the back of the bike. "Safety first."

I scowl at him. "It's going to ruin my hair."

"You'll live," he tells me, and I want to smack him.

"If you want me to ride miles across the country, we need to stop at my apartment, so I can get some stuff. I can't ride in this."

He glances down at the knee-length skirt I'm wearing, taking in the heels on my feet before bringing his gaze up to my blouse, lingering, I notice, on my tits, before he stops on my face. I cross my arms over my chest, clucking my tongue at him, letting my disapproval shine through.

"Yeah, okay."

I blink. "No fight?"

"You can't ride like that. You're right. It's okay for a short distance, but you come off the bike you're going to shred your legs."

I wait for him to climb on the bike and then I hesitate as I peer at the seat behind him, my heart hammering wildly in my chest.

"You getting on or what?" he demands over his shoulder and I snap myself out of my thoughts.

I put a foot on the pillion and throw the other one over the back of the bike with the ease of someone who has been around bikes most of their lives.

I sit slowly behind him, mindful of the fact my bare legs press against his jean-clad thighs. It feels more intimate than it has any right to be. I swallow hard and try to ignore my proximity to this man.

Without warning, he reaches out and squeezes my thigh. Electricity races through my skin at his touch and it takes everything I have not to moan.

I clamp my teeth together as he mutters, "Let's get your shit, Kitten."

This is going to be a long trip.

TWO

ROOSTER

THIS WOMAN IS ABOUT as high maintenance as they come. She's been barking orders at me since I first introduced myself in the bar and while it should piss me off, I find it weirdly attractive. I find her attractive, period. Carla is hotter than hell, with sex appeal that makes my tongue glue itself to the roof of my mouth. That hair and those pouty as fuck lips have my dick hard as a rock, and if that didn't the tattoos covering both arms certainly do. She's like every guy's wet dream, even if she has a tongue like a viper and a temper just as vicious. She gets that from Gunner. Prez has chewed me out more times than I can count over the years.

As we ride, the feel of her pressed against my back has my cock sitting up and taking notice. In the five years I've been in the club, I've never had a woman on the back of my bike, and I never planned on it either, but this situation is differ-ent. We need to travel fast and smart if we're going to make it back to New Jersey in one piece. I wasn't lying when I told her dangerous shit is going down, although I may have downplayed just how dangerous. Prez trusts me to keep his daughter safe and I'm not going to let him down. I'll protect her with my life.

She shifts behind me and I have to mentally call my dick to stand down. We're not getting any, not from her. Gunner would cut my cock off if I touch his daughter, though, danger to life has never stopped me from pursuing a woman before. I've never met a female yet who could resist my charms and even though this kitten has claws, I'm sure she's a pussy cat beneath it.

I pull up outside the apartment block she'd directed me to. The ride went too fast and I can't wait to hit the road, forty-plus hours of nothing but her and me. We'll either fuck each other senseless before we reach New Jersey, or she'll have smothered me in my sleep. Right now, it could go either way.

Her apartment is located just outside the main downtown area of Temecula, close to the bar. I'm grateful for that. I don't like her being on the bike in a skirt. If I lay the bike down, all that pretty skin on her legs is going to be one big road rash.

With such precious cargo on the back on my bike I take it slower than I would usually, carefully navigating the traffic. Luckily, the late hour means there isn't a lot of it, but all it takes is for one cage driver to take their eye off the ball for us to end up roadkill. I love riding, but it comes with dangers.

Her apartment block is a modern looking building that doesn't look like it has great security, which pisses me off. Carla is a club princess. She should be somewhere safe. What the hell is Gunner thinking letting her live somewhere like this?

I growl a curse under my breath as I cut the engine on the bike, both my boots placed on the asphalt.

"What's your problem now?" She huffs as she climbs off

the back and starts to undo the helmet. As soon as her hair is free, her hand goes to her flattened curls. She still looks beautiful, even without the volume of her hair.

"Ain't got a problem," I tell her, watching the movement of her hands.

"Why are you growling then?"

I scowl and kick down the stand before climbing off the back myself. I check my bike is secure before I turn back to her, tugging the bandanna off my face and pulling my helmet off.

"Where's the security, Kitten?"

"Why would I need security? And stop calling me Kitten. My name is Carla."

I grin at her before I sober. "Your pops know you're living in a place without locked gates on the front?"

"My father knows what I want him to know. I'm not sixteen, Rooster. I don't answer to him."

I snort. She may think that, but we all answer to Gunner in the end.

I follow her as she strides over to the front door of the ground floor apartment—another tick in the shitty security box—and I lean against the wall by the door as she slips her key into the lock.

She steps into the apartment first and I move in behind her, my eyes everywhere. Inside is nothing like I imagined. The décor screams old, and I don't mean falling into deprivation, I mean everything is vintage. The couch is in the style of the nineteen-thirties and there's old posters on the wall from the war. Pinup models who share a similar hairstyle to hers are in frames lining the back wall. It's like I've stepped into a time capsule. It's stylish as fuck, though, not that I know jack about style, but I can tell a lot of thought went into the decoration.

"This is a hell of a place you've got," I tell her.

Carla's eyes find mine as I finish sweeping the room and a little pink infuses her cheeks. After a moment, she tears her gaze away and I feel my lips pull up into a smirk. Yeah, she's interested, even if she's pretending she's not.

"Thanks."

I shove my hands into my jeans' pockets. "Pack light," I say. "Ain't room on the bike for whatever girly shit you want to bring. One bag. That's it."

Her eyes roll. "I don't have 'girly shit'. I have necessities."

I sigh. This might be harder than I thought. "Make sure your 'necessities' fit into one bag."

I watch as she crosses her arms under her tits, my eyes gravitating there of their own volition. I'm only human. Tits are tits and when they're in my eye line…

She clears her throat and I lift my eyes. "My face is up here, pervert."

I grin at her. Busted. "Go and pack. I want to make it at least a couple of hours before we find somewhere to stay for the night."

"It's late. Are you going to be okay to ride?"

"For a moment there, it sounds like you care about me."

"Don't hold your breath."

I laugh. "Being on the back of a bike is second nature to me. As soon as I start getting tired, we can stop for the night."

She sighs loudly and disappears up the small hallway toward what I assume is the bedroom.

I peer around for a moment, before I sink onto her couch. It might look nice, but it's the most uncomfortable thing I've ever sat on. Couches are built to feel good, to relax on. I don't understand how anyone could ever get comfortable on this thing. It's like a torture device.

In the end, I just perch my ass on the edge of the cushion.

"You need a new couch, Kitten. This thing is an abomination to couches."

"What?" she yells from the bedroom.

"Your couch is shit."

Her head pops around the door, scowling at me. "No one asked you to sit on it."

"You want me to stand?"

"Honestly, I'd rather you weren't here at all, yet here you are."

I put a hand to my chest. "Ouch, that hurt."

She scoffs, rolling her eyes skyward. "Like you can be hurt."

I smirk at her, but I have the feeling she could be the only person capable of causing knife wounds in my skin.

"You packed?"

"I was halfway through when you started complaining about my couch." She disappears back into the bedroom and doesn't come out for another ten minutes. I've studied every inch of her living area in that time. It's fussy as hell, but I do like that there's something new to find every time you look.

When she steps back into the room, I push to my feet. Surprisingly, she did as I asked and managed to get all her shit into one small bag. I'm amazed. I really thought we'd be arguing about lightening her load.

"Ready?"

"As I'll ever be," she mutters.

"Kitten, this is going to be a long trip if you don't lighten up."

"If you're expecting me to lighten up you're going to be waiting a long time. I don't want to come on this trip. I have no interest in going back to Jersey. I just wanted to live my life in peace, free from bikers and drama. Is that too much to ask?"

This woman...

I let my lips lift at the corners. "When you pull that stick out of your ass, make sure you let me know." She fires me a death glare, which I ignore. "Come on, let's hit the road."

She looks like she'd rather do anything but, although she does follow me out, and I can't help but wonder if we're going to survive the next few days.

THREE

CARLA

I HATE HIM. I hate his breathing guts. The man is obnoxious, full of himself and okay, he might have reason to be considering he looks like he does, but that's not the point. I want to throttle him even as I want to scale him like a tree. My hormones are all over the place.

I watch as he fastens my bag to the back of the bike, the thick muscles in his arms bunching as he moves. He's sexy as hell, but the man knows it, which isn't attractive, but even so, I can't stop watching him.

I have a problem.

When he's done, he turns back to me and I clamp my jaw shut. I wonder if I was drooling too.

He grins, as if he knows where my thoughts have gone and my mouth pulls into a scowl.

Jackass.

I fasten my helmet and check my jeans are tucked properly into my boots. The last thing we need is for a loose piece of clothing to get caught while we're riding. When I'm sure everything is okay, I pull the zipper up on my leather biker jacket. It's a warm evening, but on the back of the bike, it'll get cold after a little while.

Rooster roams his eyes over me, lingering over the narrow set of my waist before he rubs a thumb over his lips.

"A biker's fucking dream," he mutters and I roll my eyes.

"Yeah, it'll definitely be in your dreams."

He climbs onto the bike, making a big show of cocking his leg over the back. This man... he's crazy. Why on earth did my father send him? Of all the bikers in his club...

He could have sent Grim or Bullet. Anyone would be better than this asshole. I'd rather spend the next few days with one of the club bunnies, women who sleep with the brothers on the regular, than put up with this brazen biker.

"You getting on?" he demands when I don't make any move to get on behind him.

What the hell am I getting myself into?

I sigh and move over to the bike. I climb on the back, using his shoulders to steady myself, ignoring the electricity that whizzes through me as I touch him. I'm not even going to think about it, because thinking about it would mean admitting I feel something for this man, and I absolutely do not.

Nope.

As soon as I'm seated behind him, he glances over his shoulder at me, giving me a grin. He turns back around and starts the bike up, the rumbling of the engine vibrating through me, the roar of the pipes loud. Without invitation, he reaches behind him and grabs my hands, pulling them around his waist.

"Let go," I hiss at him, but he just chuckles.

"Retract the claws, Kitten. I'm not trying to get into your panties, but this is safer than traveling with you hanging onto the bitch bar at the back."

"Says who?" I demand, trying to pull my hands free, but his hold on my wrists is like iron shackles around me.

"Says me. We're going to be hitting speed when we get onto the highway. I need to know you're going to be safe sitting behind me."

I give up trying to free my hands and sigh loudly. "Fine. Let's just get this over with."

"You don't sound excited about this road trip."

I lean forward and hiss in his ear, "Let's get one thing straight, Rooster. I'm only sitting behind you because I have no choice. I'd rather walk than have to touch you."

"Ouch, that was a shot to the heart." I can hear the laughter in his voice and it makes me want to strangle him.

"Has anyone ever told you you're the most infuriating man on the planet?"

"It's come up in conversation a few times," he admits.

"I'd say I'm surprised, but I'm not."

He laughs before he hits the gas and we take off. I try not to lean into his back, but with the wind whipping at us, I have to duck behind him to protect myself. I should have put a bandanna on.

The roads are quiet because of the late hour, lit only by the streetlights. As we get on the I-10 and head east, I find the tension leaching out of my shoulders and I relax, enjoying the ride. It's been a long time since I was last on the back of a Harley and I forgot how freeing, how amazing it feels. It's like flying. It makes all the ugly thoughts, all my worries dissipate—for a time, at least.

I can't help but worry about my father and if he's okay. What is going on that is so bad I need to come home? In the six years I've been away from home, he's never once demanded I come back to New Jersey, which makes me think whatever is happening is really bad, and that makes panic flare through my stomach. The thought of my father in danger sends knife pricks along my spine. He's all I have left. My mom did a Houdini on us when I was just a few months old. She didn't want a kid and was happy to leave my dad to raise me. It's always been the two of us, which makes me feel like the worst daughter for staying away all these years. He sacrificed so much for me. I should have done better. I was wrapped up in my own needs, though, my own feelings. I never stopped to consider how my actions might hurt my father. I didn't stop to consider what leaving did to him. Now, it could be too late.

I want to interrogate Rooster, find out what the danger is, but there's no way of talking on the back of the bike, so all I can do is enjoy the ride.

By the time we pass Palm Desert, palm trees lining sections of the road, I'm starting to get tired. I don't know how Rooster is still riding, but he manages another nearly two hours before he pulls off the I-10 and finds a motel just off the highway in a place called Blythe. It's right on the California-Arizona border.

He pulls into a space in front of the reception and kicks down the stand. I climb off, my legs feeling like jello. We must have been on the road for at least three hours, maybe more and my body is feeling it. I'm cold and I'm aching. I can't help but think flying would have been easier than this.

When I wobble, he reaches out to steady me.

"Easy, Kitten."

"My legs are numb," I complain, which makes him chuckle. "Are your legs numb?"

"I'm used to riding."

How the hell anyone can be used to riding like that for hours, I'll never know.

I watch as he climbs off the bike and undoes his helmet. He has helmet hair, which would make me laugh except I'm sure my own looks horrible, too.

"Come on, let's go book a room."

He places both our helmets on the back of the bike and together we head into the office. There's a rangy looking guy behind the counter who eyes us like we're there to rob the place. Bikers get a bad rap, but considering Rooster isn't even wearing his cut, I find the man's attitude annoying.

"Can we get a twin room for the night?" Rooster asks.

The guy eyes him then moves over to the computer. After typing for a couple of seconds, he mutters, "Going to need a credit card."

Rooster pulls out a card from his wallet and slides it over the counter. The thought of a biker having a credit rating almost has me laughing, but I manage to hold it back.

He pays for the room and the man hands him a key.

"Has anyone ever told you you're a real people person?" Rooster asks as he slides his card back into his wallet. It disappears into his ass pocket.

The man grunts and Rooster grins as I stifle a laugh. "Really, your conversational skills are top notch."

He eyes Rooster. "You need something else?"

"I'd suggest some hospitality, but I think that's a losing battle." He turns to me. "Come on, Kitten."

His hand comes to the small of my back and I feel the heat of his hand burning through my skin. I should pull away, but I can't bring myself to. He feels good against me.

He gets our bags off the back of the bike before he directs me towards room number six and when he moves his hand to open the door, I feel the loss of his touch.

He steps inside, hitting the lights. It floods the space, which is clean, although basic. Not that we need much. There's two twin doubles and a dresser. A bathroom sits off the main room. The carpet is brown, worn, but clean.

Rooster moves to the window and tugs the curtains over,

shutting out any prying eyes while I sink onto the edge of the bed. I remove my boots, wiggling my toes when they're free.

"That was a long assed ride."

"Yeah, but we'll have less far to go tomorrow. You want to use the bathroom first?"

I shake my head. "You go."

He shrugs and heads into the room. I listen as the shower starts up. He's naked in there.

My mouth dries and my eyes linger on the door. I may dislike him, but I'm not immune to those good looks or that dimple.

I'm flicking through the television channels, trying to distract my mind when he steps out of the bathroom, a white towel slung around his hips. My eyes move to his abs, and what abs they are. The guy doesn't quite have a six pack, but it's not far off, and his chest is inked with different designs I want to study. He's hotter than Hades and my body is reacting to him, whether I want it to or not.

I'm in so much trouble.

FOUR

ROOSTER

SHE'S STARING at my body like I'm a piece of prized meat. I grin. I knew she wasn't immune to me. When I catch her staring at my chest, I can't stop from firing back her own words at her.

"My face is up here, pervert."

Her eyes snap to mine before she scowls, her mouth pulling into a tight line. I can see how much I'm getting under her skin, but for some reason, I enjoy the banter between us.

"Believe me, you've got nothing I'm interested in."

"I would believe you, except you were ogling me."

She splutters and shakes her head. "I was not."

Her attention goes back to the television, but she's not really focused on it. I can tell by the way she keeps casting me side-long glances.

"Woman, your eyes were all over my body." I put my hand to my chest. "I'm not just a pretty face, you know? I've got feelings."

This makes her snort her disbelief, which makes my smirk widen.

"I know exactly who you are, Rooster."

"And who's that?"

Carla turns to face me, her eyes blazing fire. "You're the type of man who thinks he can get what he wants with just a few honeyed words or a look."

She's got me sussed completely. I am that guy, but it usually works. I've used this method of getting what I want for years. She's proving tough to crack.

"That's not all I am."

Her eyes nearly roll out of her head. "I figured you out the moment you sat down at my bar. I knew exactly who you were and what you were about. That view hasn't changed. You're a cocky bastard with no regard for anything but getting what you want, and I'm not 'on the menu'." There's a lot of derision in her words. There's also a lot to unpack there. "Look, I get it I need to go home. I'm going, willingly—"

"Debatable," I mutter.

"—but that doesn't mean we need to talk or pretend to be friends."

"Who's pretending? I thought we were friends."

Her eyes narrow and I'm pretty sure she's considering kicking me in the balls. "Can you be serious for five seconds?"

"I don't know. I've never tried."

She throws her hands up into the air, exasperation in the movement. "The only way we'll survive the next few days without killing each other is if we just don't talk."

My stomach clenches at this idea. The thought of not speaking to this woman doesn't sit right with me at all. I like talking to her. I like tormenting her is probably a better assessment.

Maybe she's right about not talking...

I move over to my bag and rummage inside, looking for some clean underwear. "This is going to be a very dull trip if we can't speak to each other, Kitten."

"And stop calling me that!"

"You don't like it?" I ask, keeping my voice level.

"You know I don't."

"You need to learn to relax. You're definitely Gunner's kid. He's just as uptight—"

"I am not uptight," she snaps. "At least I'm not usually. You bring this out in me."

"Are you trying to say I'm irritating."

I pull out a pair of boxer briefs and have the satisfaction of watching as her eyes slide to them. Yeah, she's interested. I've never had a woman show me she's keen with so much anger, though. This is a new one on me.

"What do you think?"

I flash her one of my patented shit-eating grins, then without another word, I step back into the bathroom, closing the door behind me. I can't figure this woman out at all. She spits such bile at me, but then she's staring at me like I'm her next meal. I don't understand where her head is at. Does she like me or not? Does she want me or not? I'm not sure she knows herself.

I quickly dry off and pull my boxers on. I gather up my clothes and step out of the room to find her still sitting on the bed, eyes glued to the TV. I'm not even sure what she's watching. It looks like some old cop show, but what the hell it is, I don't know.

Her eyes slide to me as I toss my clothes on the chair at the side of the bed.

"Where are the rest of your clothes?" she demands, covering her eyes.

I glance down my bare chest to my boxers. Nothing has

slipped out. I bring my gaze back to her, not sure what the hell her problem is.

"I sleep naked usually. Count your lucky stars I put on something."

Carla's eyes flare. "You are not sleeping naked in the same room as me."

Her eye rolling must be catching because mine go skyward. "Relax. Your virtue is safe."

"I'm not worried about my virtue. I just don't want to see anything."

I stare at her a beat. "You know, looking at you, dressing the way you do, I didn't expect you to be a prude."

I know my words are the wrong thing to say when her eyes narrow, flames dancing in their depths.

"What the hell does that mean? Dressing the way I do."

Oh, boy. I really stepped into that hornet's nest.

"I just meant you look a lot more fun than you actually are, Kitten."

"I'm fun."

I snort. "You are the absolute opposite of fun."

She pushes off the bed and snags her bag from the foot of it and without a word storms into the bathroom.

I grin. Yeah, this is going to be a fun few days. She might kill me in my sleep. She might kill me while I'm awake too. Carla doesn't seem to like me very much.

The sound of the shower coming on has my cock stirring in my boxers. The thought of her in there, naked, the water cascading over her is enticing.

I ignore the way my mind is going and check the front door is locked before climbing into the bed nearest it. I pull my phone out. There are no messages from Gunner or Grim, which is both a good thing, but also concerns me. Have the Filthy Reapers attacked already? Are we riding into a war zone?

No, Gunner would have found a way to let me know not to bring his daughter home if their club had attacked ours. There's no way in hell he'd let me take her anywhere into danger. If the clubhouse hadn't been under threat, the whole club would have ridden west to get her, but that wasn't an option. It would have meant leaving our territory undefended. It was a decision that killed my president, but sending me alone was and remains the right decision. Too many bikers would draw attention. One lone rider is more inconspicuous, able to blend better.

I fire off a text message to Gunner and get a reply back almost immediately telling me everything is quiet at home. Thank fuck.

I hear the water shut off and it's torture imagining her gorgeous curves as she steps out of the shower. I need to clamp down on those thoughts, though. Gunner will gut me if I touch his daughter. It'll be the last free breath I take.

She steps out of the bathroom in a cloud of steam a few moments later dressed in tiny sleep shorts that show so much leg and a little camisole top that does nothing to hide the fact she's not wearing a bra.

I lied.

This is torture. This is the worst. I try not to ogle her, but hell, I'm only human. I can't stop from looking at that rocking body she has. She's stunningly beautiful, even with a towel wrapped around her hair.

Carla moves over to the bed and sits on the edge.

I keep my eyes locked on the television, which I didn't turn off. I'm grateful as fuck because if I look at her, I might explode in my boxers. She looks stunning with all that makeup wiped off her face, although she looks beautiful with it on too. The woman is just the picture of perfection.

I try not to watch as she unravels the towel from her hair and begins to dry it. I try not to stare at the slopes of her shoulders. Her expansive curls are gone, but I prefer this natural look. She looks beautiful.

I pull my eyes away and concentrate on the TV. It is going to be a long fucking night.

FIVE

CARLA

I WAKE unsure where I am for a moment. Then I remember the motel we stopped in when we hit Blythe yesterday. I also remember I'm sharing a room with a certain brazen biker.

Slowly, I turn over and when I do, I'm greeted with a view of his ass. He's somehow kicked most of the covers off and is tangled around the comforter, his ass hanging out showcasing the perfect globes in his boxer briefs. My mouth dries instantly and my tongue feels too thick for my mouth. He looks delicious and I curse myself for thinking that. I'm not supposed to be interested in a crazy assed biker, especially one who thinks he's God's gift to women, but I can't deny he makes my belly flip a little.

I get out of bed and head into the bathroom to clean my teeth, freshen up and get dressed. I pull on a pair of riding jeans, a tee and my boots. I don't have any of my hair stuff with me, not that I could put my hair in curls anyway. The helmet will destroy any styling, so instead, I braid it. At least that way it'll stay neat and I won't look like a tree.

By the time I step out of the bathroom, Rooster is sitting on the edge of the bed, facing the motel door. His broad

27

shoulders are muscled and arced between them is the words Savage Riders. I swallow hard. How does he have the power to make me forget who he really is, the danger that comes with his lifestyle? A danger that he can't avoid. Even now, I'm being dragged thousands of miles across the US because they're knee-deep in trouble.

I clear my throat, and he twists to look over his shoulder at me. His eyes move up and down my body in a way that makes me internally squirm before they come to rest on my face.

"Morning, sunshine. It's about a two-hour ride to Phoenix. Figured we'd stop there for breakfast, unless you can't wait that long."

"No, it's fine. Although if we stop every two hours, it's going to take us a month to reach New Jersey," I tell him.

He smirks. "Think of all the fun we could get up to in a month."

I shake my head. "Think all you like. Nothing is ever going to happen between us."

"We'll see, Kitten," is his infuriating response.

He finishes getting dressed and we gather up our stuff, ready to leave the motel. It's hotter than Hades already, even though it's only early in the morning, and the sun is beaming down on us. The desert landscape stretches before us, trees lining the road, a hint of mountains on the distant horizon towards the Arizona border. There are a few clouds in the sky, which is such a bright blue it doesn't look entirely real. Dust settles in the back of my throat as the breeze picks up a little, cooling me.

Rooster takes the key back to the motel reception while I wait by the bike. When he steps out of the building, I can't help but follow his movements. The man knows how to swagger and he moves with the confidence of a person who has never been challenged in his entire life. There is something attractive about that and I can't lie and say I'm not affected, because I am. He makes my stomach dip, makes me feel things I shouldn't. I don't know what to do with this. I don't want a biker, never have, but right now, I'm thinking things about Rooster I really shouldn't be thinking.

I lick my suddenly dry lips and swallow hard as he approaches, trying not to let on that I'm affected by him.

"Ready?" I ask.

He nods and pulls his keys from the wallet chain slung around his hip and upper thigh. I watch as he detaches them from the chain and pushes them into the ignition. He then reaches for his helmet as I reach for mine and a jolt of electricity goes through me as we brush our hands over each other's. I peer up at him and see need in his eyes, desire, want. Butterflies flutter against my stomach, their frenetic wing beats sending tingles of pleasure through me. I pull my hand away and lower my eyes, not wanting him to see I'm affected.

My heart starts to gallop in my chest and I don't understand why. The man is infuriating. Everything about him drives me crazy, yet I can't deny he's attractive.

I watch as he throws a jean-clad leg over the back of the bike and waits for me to climb on behind him. I quickly fasten my helmet and climb on. When I'm settled, his hand goes to my thigh and I try to ignore how that ignites fire inside me.

When he starts the engine up, I'm nearly panting. It takes everything I have not to. I secure my hands around his waist and he maneuvers the bike toward the exit.

Then we're back on the I-10 and moving at speed through the desert. As we pass the Arizona border sign, I can't stop the sinking feeling in the pit of my stomach. I vowed I'd never go back to Jersey, and yet here I am, taking the nearly three-thousand-mile journey back home.

I press into Rooster's back, my heart feeling heavy as we ride, the wind whipping past us both.

For miles, civilization is pretty sparse until we hit the outskirts of Phoenix. It's almost a relief to see signs of life again. Rooster directs the bike off the highway and into the city center. He stops at the first diner we come across, a small mom and pop type place that looks clean and inviting.

He pulls the bike into a space and waits for me to climb off. Once my feet are on the asphalt, he kicks the stand down and gets off himself.

I've never been to Phoenix, so my eyes are everywhere, taking in everything as we stride into the diner. It seems open, more sprawling than most cities. The buildings are spread out, giving it an airy feeling, despite the fact it's a huge place. The traffic moves on the main street as I wait for Rooster to get himself sorted.

Then together we head inside the diner. It's decorated in red and white, with individual booths lining the window side and there are stools at the counter. Rooster leads us to a booth near the back and sits facing the doors, leaving me to sit with my back to them. He picks up a menu, his eyes moving around the space. It seems casual, but there's a sharpness in his gaze that tells me he's seeing everything. I glance over my shoulder before bringing my eyes back to him.

"Everything okay?"

He beams at me, his smile radiant, his dimple sneaking out. "Yeah." He hands me the other menu. "Pick whatever you want. I'm paying."

I arch a brow. "Why are you paying? I have money."

His eyes lift to mine. "Kitten, do you enjoy arguing with me for the sake of it?"

I fold my arms on the table top. "No, but I don't need you to take care of me, Rooster. I can look after myself."

"Can we try to have breakfast without an argument?"

I huff out a breath. "Fine. If you're so set on paying, be my guest."

My gaze roam over the menu. I can feel his eyes on me, so I raise my head to find he is staring at me.

"What?"

"You're cute when you're huffy."

I let out another sigh and peer back at the menu. "And you're annoying, but who's keeping track?"

The waitress comes over, putting a halt to our conversation. She's maybe in her thirties, pretty, with blonde hair that's pulled up into a loose ponytail. I sit back, expecting Rooster to flirt with her, since he seems to like anything in a skirt, but he keeps his eyes locked on me as he orders.

I should look away, but I can't.

I rattle off my own order without looking away and when the waitress leaves the table, Rooster leans his arms on it and gets close to my face.

"I think you put on a good show, Kitten, but deep down, I think you like me. I think you more than like me, and I'm going to spend the rest of this trip showing you how much."

SIX

ROOSTER

CARLA WRINKLES her nose at my words and I have to resist the urge to laugh. She's so desperate to hate me, she can't see the truth right in front of her. She does like me—although I'm not sure if that is romantically or not. That might take longer to unpack.

"I don't think so, but nice try Romeo." She reaches for a napkin and picks at the edges of it, shredding pieces of it onto the table.

I grab her hands, cupping them in mine, stopping her destruction. She raises her gaze to me and for a moment, I get lost in those big eyes of hers.

"You'll see," I repeat my earlier sentiment.

Tugging her hands from under mine, she puts them on her lap instead, under the table, away from my reach. I grin.

"What are you smirking about?" she demands, sounding annoyed.

"Nothing, Kitten. Absolutely nothing."

Her eyes narrow on me, shooting daggers in my direction before her fingers move to the end of her braid. I loved her pinup look, but this shit is hotter than hell too. She looks sexy as sin, and I want to have her, but I want her to want me too, which might prove a challenge. Right now, she swings between heated, needy gazes and firing flames at me.

Our breakfast is brought out, silencing her as the waitress places a plate in front of each of us. She digs in first, and the moment the pancake touches her tongue, she moans.

"They're amazing."

They might be, but that noise she made has my cock sitting up and taking notice. Would that be the noise she'd make while I was inside her? I swallow hard, trying to regain control of my body, which seems to have its own ideas.

"Glad we stopped then," I tell her, genuinely meaning it. "Although we should have taken the I-15 and stopped at Vegas instead."

Her brows crawl up her forehead. "I don't think putting you anywhere near Las Vegas would be a good idea."

"I'm an excellent poker player."

"You'd get lost at the tables and we'd never make it back to Jersey."

I tilt my head at her, my smile broad. "You act like you know everything about me."

"I know enough."

"Your father gave me an order to bring you home. That's what I'm going to do, no matter what, but he didn't say we couldn't have fun on the way."

She grabs another forkful of pancake. "This is what you call this? Fun?"

"I think if you relaxed for a moment and enjoyed it for what it is, you'd get a lot more out of this trip."

Carla stares at me a beat, chewing as she does. Once she's emptied her mouth, she says, "What's your name?"

I dig into my own breakfast, taking a generous helping of pancake and bacon. "Rooster. Didn't we go over this already?"

Her eyes roll. "I mean your real name, asshole."

"Why?"

"Rooster's a stupid name."

"Blame the club. They gave it to me."

"So, what is it?"

I don't know why, but the thought of her having my real name and calling me by it has a tingle of excitement racing through me.

"It's Finn Reilly."

"Finn." She rolls the letters off her tongue in a sultry way. "You don't like your name?"

I shrug. "I don't care either way, but I've been Rooster for so long now, I don't know how to be anyone else."

"Why did you join the Savage Riders?"

My eyes go to the window, peering out over the parking lot to the street beyond. Cars are moving, but there's a lot of traffic.

"That's a complicated question with a complicated answer."

I watch as Carla sits back in her seat and shrugs. "We have time."

I let out a breath. "I didn't grow up with much. My dad was an alcoholic. My mom did her best, but she was a single parent with three kids, trying to keep money coming in that he was pissing away every night. When I turned eighteen, I was rudderless. I had no idea how to do shit, but I knew I wanted a better life for any kids I might have."

"So, you joined an MC?" Her brow arches. "Not seeing how that's a better life."

"I earn good money. Enough to provide for a family. I have my own house that I own outright, a decent car, my bike and plenty of savings. I take care of the people who mean something to me. My mom included in that."

Her face softens. "You take care of your mom?"

I shrug. "Least I can do. She sacrificed everything for us growing up."

I know Carla's mom took off when she was a kid. Gunner's mentioned it before, so I don't bring up her mom, in case it's still a sore point for her.

"You're not supposed to be like this," she mutters.

"Like what?"

"Someone who cares about his mom. You're supposed to be a jerk."

"I can still be that," I say, waggling my eyebrows.

She rolls her eyes, but she laughs as she does. Breakthrough? I'm not holding my breath, but it definitely seems more positive than shooting venom at me, which is her usual go to.

"Your mom lives in New Jersey?"

"About twenty minutes from the clubhouse."

"You have two siblings?"

"Younger sisters."

"You take care of them too?" she asks on an arched brow.

"When they need it, yeah."

She throws her head back, so she's looking at the ceiling. "Stop being a good guy. It makes it harder to hate you."

I take a sip of my coffee, washing down my food. "You know you don't have to hate me. It ain't mandatory."

"You're a biker."

"I'm also a lot more than that."

Her eyes soften. "I'm starting to see that."

When we're finished, we step out of the booth. I drop some cash on the table and give the waitress a lift of my chin as I steer Carla toward the doors. My hand automatically goes to the small of her back, but she doesn't move away or try to stop me touching her. I take that as another uptick in the progress column.

The sun is beating down as we step over to the bike, the

heat so dry it steals all the moisture from the air. I wipe at my forehead, which is already beading with sweat. Carla folds her jacket and places it in her bag. It's too hot to ride with it on, and it's only going to get hotter as the day goes on.

I climb on the back of the bike and she gets on behind me without hesitation. Our ride takes us through the Tonto National Forest, which is surrounded by mountains and rocks. There's green among the dusty landscape, but it blends so well with the surroundings, it doesn't lend much color to the horizon.

Carla clings to my back, her chin resting on my shoulder as we ride. I love the feel of her at my back, more than I'd probably care to admit. I feel whole, complete with her sitting behind me. I just have to make her see I'm worth taking a chance on, while avoiding the wrath of her father.

SEVEN

CARLA

WE HIT the New Mexico border after what feels like forever and head toward Albuquerque. We have to stop on the way, both of us feeling the heat. Needing to get out of it, we stop in a small town called Gallup. Hours in the Arizona then New Mexico sun is giving me a headache.

Rooster finds us a motel with a pool—thank you, Google —and we stop at a store to buy suits before we ride over there. The place looks clean, but basic, and when he kicks the stand down, I climb off the back, ignoring the trembling in my legs.

I don't even complain about how long this journey is going to take if we keep stopping because I'm desperate to use that pool. I'm so hot, I feel like I might expire.

"You know, this would have been easier if we just flew," I mutter as I pull my helmet off.

"Don't trust planes," is his bizarre response.

"You don't trust planes?"

"Only thing I trust is my bike, Kitten. This is taking longer, but look at the experience we're having. I'm guessing you ain't ever seen our beautiful country like we're seeing it now."

"I'd be just as happy seeing it from the air," I grumble, wiping the dust off my jeans.

"Yeah, but I can't carry my gun on a flight."

This admission stops me in my tracks. "You're carrying?"

He turns and looks at me, and I see something dark pass across his eyes before it fades. "Can't be too careful."

"You think the danger is that bad?"

"I think it's bad enough your dad wanted you home, where he can protect you, Carla."

His voice is serious and that freaks me out. The man hasn't been serious once in the whole time we've been together.

"Are they going to hurt my dad?"

He stares at me then says, "Not if the club can help it."

"Who are these people? Why are they a threat?"

"Can't tell you. It's club business, Kitten, but we're handling it, I promise you that."

Anger floods my veins, burning a path around my body. "Don't feed me that bullshit line. Tell me."

He sighs, brushing his hair back from his face, his other hand clutching his helmet.

"It doesn't work like that. You know it doesn't."

I do, but still I push him. "You're dragging me across the country. I might lose my job. You owe me the truth."

His eyes crawl over my face before he says, "Let's go and check-in."

Frustration gnaws at my gut. "Rooster!"

"Darlin', I can't tell you, and even if I could I wouldn't, because it ain't for you to worry your pretty little head about."

Disbelief has me scoffing. "I can't believe you just said that, you jerk."

I storm off in the direction of the office, not wanting to even speak to him. What an asshole. I hear his heavy motorcycle boots following after me as I drag open the reception door and step into a wall of air conditioning. It's divine. Cold air licks up my heated skin, cooling me instantly.

I stand to one side as Rooster handles checking us in and then I move out of the building, back into the heat and toward the bike. I barely make it two steps before his fingers circle around my wrist, pulling me up short.

"Kitten…" Warning cracks through the name.

I ignore it. I tug my hand away, my rage flaring.

"Don't 'Kitten' me."

"You know I can't tell you this shit and you know why. You grew up in this life. You ain't naïve to the way it works."

He's right. I'm not, but frustration over the rules makes me tetchy as hell. I want to throttle him for throwing that club business line at me. I'm not club and I shouldn't be treated like I have to follow their stupid archaic ways.

"This involves me. You should tell me what danger I'm in."

"You do as you're told and there won't be any danger."

I grit my teeth. "I want to use the pool."

My change in direction has him huffing, but he doesn't call me on it as he unhooks our bags from the back of the bike and carries it over to the room we were given.

We both take a quick shower, neither of us speaking to each other, and then put on our suits. My bikini is a little tight, but nothing is hanging out, so I don't worry about it.

When he steps out of the bathroom in his board shorts, I can't stop my eyes from gravitating toward his body. It should be illegal to be this good looking.

I clear my throat and grab a couple of towels from the bathroom and make my way outside to the pool. There are a couple of loungers, so I drag one under the parasol and lay the towel on top of it. Rooster moves the other, although I wish he wouldn't. I don't want to sit near him.

I leave my phone on my lounger and climb into the pool. The water is cool, the sun heating it enough to make it comfortable to get into. Instantly, the heat leaches right from my skin as the water skims over me.

Rooster isn't as careful about getting in. He runs and cannonballs himself, splashing water over me. When he surfaces, he runs his fingers through his wet hair, pushing it out of his face. I splash him.

"Asshole," I mutter.

He splashes me back. "If you're scared of a bit of water, you probably shouldn't be in the pool."

I splash him again. "I'm not scared, jerk. You just didn't have to spray water all over me."

He grins and I'm soaked again. Then I'm pulled into his arms, my mouth inches from his, my eyes peering up into his. I forget how to breathe, how to think, how to do anything but stare at him. He is extraordinarily handsome, I can't deny that, and I can't deny that he affects me either, because he does. Our bodies are nearly touching and I want to move that few inches and close the gap, but I don't. I can't. Even when his fingers move to cup my jaw, I hold my ground.

"You're the most beautifully infuriating woman on the planet," he murmurs, his eyes crawling over my face. "I've never met anyone quite like you."

"That goes both ways," I tell him on a breath, unable to tear my eyes away.

I think he's going to kiss me, but then a car backfires and his gaze snaps away, his whole body tensing as he pushes me behind him. When he's sure there's no threat, he moves to the edge of the pool and climbs out.

"You've got twenty minutes in there, then we're hitting the road again."

I frown at him. "We're not staying overnight?"

"No," he fires back.

"Why'd you bother with the room?" I demand, exasperation making my voice pitched higher than usual.

"Thought it would be safe. It ain't." He sits on the edge of the lounger and reaches under his towel. I see the glint of metal and realize he brought the gun out with him.

Dread rolls through me. I let my guard down for a little while, but I need to remember this trip isn't for pleasure and that he's here only to keep my ass alive while we travel to New Jersey.

EIGHT

ROOSTER

I NEED to stop looking at this as a trip. I'm here to keep Carla safe and nothing else, but hell, when I'm with her I want it to be so much more. It can't be, though. That car backfiring reminded me of the real and very present danger we're facing.

What if that had been a gun?

What if I hadn't managed to protect her in time?

I don't think the Filthy Reapers have followed me to Temecula, but I have no clue what those freaks are capable of.

We shouldn't keep stopping so much, but the heat was unbearable and I didn't have a choice. I could feel the blazing heat coming off her through the back of my tee and honestly, I was worried she might get sunstroke. I was feeling a little woozy myself, but watching her splashing about in the pool, I can't bring myself to force her to leave.

I peer down at the towel that hides my gun. I can protect her and I will protect her with my dying breath, but that means keeping my eye on the ball and not letting my attention wander. I've been too lax with her safety.

"Time to go," I tell her, my voice gruff.

I expect an argument, but she doesn't give me one. I wonder for a moment if I've scared her. My thoughts obliterate as she climbs out of the pool looking like every guy's wet dream. Her bikini clings to her wet body like a second skin, her nipples poking out of the material tantalizingly. My mouth waters as droplets run down between her ample tits. Her sleeves of tattoos look amazing against the black of the suit. Carla looks stunning, period.

"Anyone ever tell you you're a killjoy?" she asks as she steps up to me and reaches for a towel. My eyes follow the movement as she dabs it between her breasts.

"Better that than one of us getting shot," I mutter and pull myself out of my daze. Quickly, I gather up our shit and trail after her. I hate to drag her away from here, especially when she seems like she's having so much fun, and fun isn't something Carla seemed to care much about until today, but this isn't a holiday, and I need to remember that.

My eyes are everywhere as we head back toward the room, seeking potential threats, but there's no one around and everything is blissfully quiet apart from the dull moan of the traffic in the distance from the highway.

As soon as the motel door is shut behind us, Carla speaks.

"You're worried." It's a statement rather than a question.

"I have your safety to consider."

"You honestly think we're in danger out here?" she asks, grabbing one of the towels and wrapping it around her middle.

"I don't know, Kitten, and that's the problem."

She stares at me a moment. "I know you want to take care of me, but really, I'm fine. Nothing is going to happen to me, and you're right we should try to enjoy this journey."

My brow kicks up. "You want to enjoy this journey now? After all your bitching?"

She shrugs her shoulders. "You were the one who told me to."

"I know, but I didn't expect you'd want to."

She surprises the hell out of me by placing her hand on the side of my face, cupping my jaw.

"You'll keep us safe. I know you will."

"I'll do everything I can," I agree, "but this ain't a game, Kitten. You could die. We all could die."

Her throat works at my words and I wish I could take them back, but it's better she's prepared, better she knows the real danger she's in.

"Then we'd better get back on the road."

I let out a breath I didn't know I was holding, grateful she's not going to fight me on this and watch as she steps into the bathroom to get dressed.

I strip down in the main room and pull on my jeans, which stick to me instantly. I'd rather be in shorts right now, but riding exposed isn't the best idea. Besides, I want to put some miles between us and Gallup. Stopping there put me on edge, even though logically I knew there was no reason to be.

We hit the road mid-afternoon and blast through the rest of New Mexico, leaving Albuquerque in the rear-view mirror and heading straight for the Texas border. Night falls, the only light from the streetlamps and the headlights of the traffic moving up the highway.

Carla snuggles into my back, keeping her chin tucked against my shoulder, her arms wound around my middle. It feels amazing having her behind me, like a dream, but that dream could be shattered in an instant, so I keep my wits about me as we ride, looking out for any suspicious vehicles coming up behind us. The ride is uneventful, though, and as we cross the Texas border, I feel my eyes getting heavy. I manage to ride for another hour, until we hit Amarillo. My body then forces me to stop.

I find us a motel. It's close to the highway, so we can get straight back on it in the morning. Carla and I head into the office and she moves over to look at the tourist leaflets while I sort the room situation.

"What can I get you?" the owner asks, and I notice she pushes her tits out slightly. I have this effect on women often, so I'm used to being flirted with, but I don't want Carla to get the wrong idea, so I cast a side-long glance at her before I ask in a bored tone.

"A twin room."

She turns to the computer, her eyes fluttering at me and types something in.

"Only got one double left, sorry, sugar."

Carla steps over to us. "No way. We need two beds."

"Kitten—"

"Haven't got anything else," the woman says, a little exasperated. I don't like the tone she's using with Carla.

"We'll try another motel." Carla moves toward the door, but the woman speaks again.

"Won't have much luck. There's a convention taking place in town. Everywhere will be booked up. You're lucky I've got this room left."

Carla's teeth grind together.

"Ain't riding further, Kitten. I'm exhausted. It's just one night." I hold my hands up in supplication. "I promise, I'll keep my hands to myself."

She eyes me like she's contemplating shoving my balls up my ass.

"I'm not sharing a bed with you."

"If I had a man who looked like that," the woman mutters, "I'd chain him to my bed."

"You're welcome to him."

"This ain't my fault," I tell her. "It's a shitty situation, but it's one night and the alternative is to sleep with the bike in the parking lot."

"Fine." It looks like it takes a lot for her to say that word, but I take it as a victory.

We check-in and head to the room to dump our stuff. As soon as we step inside the room and flick the lights on Carla curses.

"That's not a double."

She's right. This bed is small. It's going to be a tight fit for the both of us.

"Parking lot," I murmur in her ear before pushing around her and stepping fully into the room. I drop our bags on the chair and sink onto the edge of the mattress. "It's not that bad."

"I don't want to share a bed with you." She pouts and it's adorable as fuck.

"I wish I could take a photograph of you right now. You look sweet as candy."

She scowls at me. "What the hell is wrong with you?"

"You're not the first person to try to figure that out, Kitten."

We find a restaurant that's still serving food and get something to eat before heading back to the motel. She's quiet through dinner, which I don't like. I try some of my best jokes on her and get nothing back, which worries me.

Carla is on edge as we get ready for bed, so I decide to let her off the hook.

"I'll sleep on the floor."

Her head snaps up and she narrows her eyes. "Why?"

"Because it's obvious you're not happy about sharing a bed with me, and I'm not a total jerk."

This makes her eyes soften, which I like more than I probably should.

"Rooster…"

I snag a pillow off the bed and toss it onto the floor.

There's not enough covers for us to both have so I lie with no blankets. I probably look pathetic lying there in just my boxer briefs

She peers down at me, her arms folding over her chest.

"I appreciate the sentiment, but this isn't going to work either. You're going to be miserable tomorrow."

I snort. "Better than you wanting to kill me."

"I don't want to kill you."

"Kitten, your claws are practically flaying me."

"We have another long day of riding tomorrow. Please, get in the bed."

I want to leap up and do as she's demanded, but I show a little restraint and don't move right away.

"Are you sure?"

Her scowl has my lips twitching. "Yes, I'm sure. Do it before I change my mind."

I climb to my feet and slip under the covers. The bed is comfortable and warm. It soothes my aching bones. I'm used to riding, but even this journey is affecting me. She must feel wrecked.

I watch as Carla hesitates for a moment then climbs under the covers. She rolls to her side, so her back is to me, as if she's trying to put a barrier between us, which makes me chuckle.

I lean over and turn the lamp off on the nightstand. Trying to sleep with her heat next to me is going to be impossible, but I turn on my side too, determined to keep my promise not to touch her.

NINE

CARLA

I WAKE with a warm body draped over me, and God, it feels good. Then I see a flash of dark hair and realize who it is.

Rooster.

I freeze, unsure what the hell to do. He's wrapped around me like a vine, his heat searing my skin where it touches. I don't want to admit how much I like this, even if I do, because nothing is ever happening between me and a biker. They are off limits.

So, why is my heart galloping in my chest and why is my breath catching as I try to draw air in?

Because you like him.

That thought scares me half to death, so I shove him off me. His eyes fly open and he peers around alert but ruffled from sleep.

"You said no touching," I hiss at him.

Realizing there's no immediate danger, the fire in his eyes dies back and he stares with hooded eyes at me.

"I didn't."

"I woke up with you practically cuddling me."

This earns me a grin that I shouldn't like, but has my stomach dipping.

"I can't help what I do in my sleep, Kitten.

I throw the covers back and climb out of bed. "This is exactly why I didn't want to share a bed—inappropriate touching!"

His eyebrows draw together, but I can see from the lift of his lips he finds this amusing.

"You really are a prude, aren't you?"

His words make my anger flare to life. "I'm not. I'm just not interested in you, so don't get any ideas, buddy."

Rooster shakes his head, chuckling. "I think the lady protests too much."

I snag my bag and storm into the bathroom. Really, I don't know what I'm so annoyed about. He's right—he can't be held accountable for what he did in his sleep—but I'm pissed I have all these unwanted feelings coming to light. I don't want to like a biker, and that puts me in a tetchy mood the entire day.

As we hit the road again, I sulk silently while sitting behind him. The desert landscape becomes greener the further we ride until we're completely surrounded by it, but the temperature is no less savage. We cross the Oklahoma border and stop in Edmond four hours after leaving Amarillo. It's late afternoon and the heat is unbearable. At least when the bike was moving, we were keeping cooler, but stopping means the sun is beating down on me and my tee is starting to stick to my body. I'm getting a tan too. Full days in the sun means my arms are starting to brown. So is Rooster, his skin turning darker than mine.

We head into the cooler shade of a deli and grill restaurant. Inside is modern, clean and the smell of the food is divine. My stomach starts rumbling as soon as we're seated.

I sit across from him, snagging the menu, just so I don't

have to talk or look at him. I'm still pissed, which I'm sure I'm exuding when he stops looking at the menu and asks me outright.

"Are you still upset about this morning?" The disbelief in his voice isn't that unsurprising. I'm acting like a brat, but the fact he brought unwanted feelings out of me is driving me batshit.

"I'm not upset," I grumble.

"You pissed because I cuddled you and you actually liked it?"

Rage fills my vision. I lean across the table and hiss in his face. "Let's get one thing straight. I am not interested in you and never will I be interested in you, so whatever dirty thoughts you have rolling around that pervert brain of yours need to stop. Last night was about necessity. I would never have willingly shared a bed with you."

He leans back and grins, his dimple coming out. "I think the problem is you do like me, and for some reason you just don't want to admit it."

"I do not."

"Kitten, you can't lie to me."

"You are the most infuriating man on the planet."

"So you've told me. I've noticed that stick up your ass is getting bigger." He leans forward over the table. "Need me to pull it out?"

I throw my hands up in the air and resist the urge to scream.

"I'm done."

"Done?"

"With this road trip. I'd rather take my chances in Temecula than ride another mile with you."

It's childish, but I push up from the table, snag my bag and storm out of the restaurant. I'm serious about walking back to California. He's such an asshole. I hate him right now. I mostly hate that what he's saying has a ring of truth to it. I do want him, and I probably do have a stick up my ass, but I don't need him to tell me about it.

"Kitten, wait up!"

His voice sounds from behind me, but I don't stop walking. I just shift my bag on my shoulder and keep my head down.

"Carla, stop." The cracked command in his voice makes my feet halt and I spin back to him.

"I would, but I'm too busy trying to remove the stick from my ass!"

He groans. "Carla—"

"No, jerk, we're done. I'm going back to Temecula."

"It ain't safe."

"It's safer than being with you. Another day with you and I'm going to end up burying you on the side of the road!" I yell into his face. He just grins, which infuriates me even more. "What are you smirking about?"

"I was just thinking how cute you are when you're mad."

"See how cute I am when I'm ripping your balls off."

"Look, I'm sorry, okay? I shouldn't have said what I did, but being infuriated works both ways, babe. You drive me nuts too."

"Thanks," I mutter, irritation rolling through me at his words.

His finger comes under my chin, forcing my gaze to meet his. "This situation is shit. I know this, but it is what it is. We can't change it. The threat to the club is very real and very dangerous, which means the threat to you is just as dire. We can't, as a club, leave a member's daughter out there unprotected. Ain't ever going to happen, Kitten. I know this life isn't one you want, but as Gunner's kid, it's the one you've got. Can't change who your pop is, can't change that you're Savage Riders' property either."

When I open my mouth to say I'm no one's property, his finger covers my mouth.

"Rules are different in our world. You've been out in the civilian one so long, you've forgotten how shit works. You're ours because your pop is ours. You'll always be family."

He's right, though I hate that he is.

"So, you coming back into the restaurant and having something to eat with me?"

I pause for so long, not sure what my answer is going to be. Then grudgingly, I nod. "Fine."

"Feel free to retract the claws a little, Kitten," he jokes and I fire him a glare.

"We're not in joking territory yet, buddy."

"No, but you will be."

Together, we walk into the restaurant and sit back at the table. He watches me carefully for a moment before he peers down at his menu.

"You know, I'm not a bad guy."

"I didn't say you were."

"I pay my taxes on time, I donate to charity. I've had my share of rescue dogs over the years."

"You have a dog?" The thought of him with a pet is almost comical to me.

"Had. He was put to sleep a few months back and I haven't had the will to get another one yet."

My heart contracts for him. It must have been so painful. I don't have pets, my lifestyle never enabled it, but I love animals.

"That must have been tough."

He stares at me a beat then sighs. "I feel like we got off on the wrong foot."

"You didn't exactly put your best foot forward."

"We're both tetchy from traveling. I think we need to just take a moment and chill out."

He's probably right. Traveling all day and sleeping in motels is not doing much for my sanity.

"I'm sorry," I tell him, meaning it. I've been a brat all day.

"You're tired. I get it. I'm tired too."

"Yeah, and you have this way of infuriating me."

"That cuts both ways, Kitten."

"I don't mean to."

"We got off on the wrong foot. Let's start again as friends, okay?"

I nod. "Friends." The word feels wrong on my tongue. What I feel for Rooster is not friendly, not even a little, and that's what scares me, because I'm falling for a biker and I shouldn't be—not if I want to keep what's left of my sanity.

TEN

CARLA

WE GET BACK on the road after our argument and ride four more hours to our next stop, Springfield, a town an hour from the Missouri border. We've crossed that many borders now I'm starting to lose track, but I'm enjoying seeing all the different landscapes as we ride. Missouri is so green compared to Arizona and New Mexico and the air smells cooler. The desert landscape felt like breathing in hell sometimes.

Springfield has an open feel with lots of red brick buildings lining the wide streets. Despite being late evening, the sun, which has yet to go down, is still warm. I'm grateful we're doing this in the summer, not the winter. I'm not sure it would be as pleasant.

We eat dinner in a small family owned restaurant we find on the main high street and then check into a hotel for the evening. Rooster might be used to riding, but I can tell this journey is taking its toll on him, and he's done it once already, coming from New Jersey to Temecula. Hitting the road again so soon is definitely taking its toll on him.

He dumps our bags by the foot of the bed and flops onto

the one nearest as soon as I shut the door behind us, boots and all.

"Maybe we should stop for a few hours tomorrow, so you can rest," I tell him, genuinely worried if he's okay. He looks exhausted.

Since we've been on the road, I've seen a different side to him—one I like. As a protector, a provider, and a genuinely good man. I didn't think he had that in him, but knowing he loves his mother, that he takes care of his sisters and that he wants to take care of me has me feeling things I shouldn't be. I can't help but be drawn to this man who is quickly becoming part of my world.

"Ain't safe to stop." He waves me off, though he doesn't move from his position on the bed.

"It's not safe to ride either when you're so tired."

He opens his eyes and comes up on his elbows to look at me. "Kitten, you actually sound worried about me."

The grin doesn't annoy me as much as it previously would have. I don't read into why that is, but I shake my head at him.

"I'm also on the back of that bike. You're risking me by being tired."

He sits up and stares at me. "I would never put you at risk. Ever."

The vehemence in his tone has my spine snapping straight. He sounds so sincere, so angry that I'd suggest otherwise.

"I know," I say quietly, and deep down I do know that.

He gets off the bed and strides toward me, his eyes blazing fire. I step backward as my spine hits the wall. His hand goes to the side of my head, pressing against the plaster.

"I would never put you at risk," he repeats. "I hope you know that."

My heart is racing, galloping a hundred miles per hour in

my chest, and my breath is coming out in ragged pants. This close up, I can see the flecks in his eyes, can see the way his pupils have dilated, and I can see the hunger.

He wants me, and the thing is, I want him too.

His eyes crawl my face and all the air freezes in my lungs as he dips his head and his mouth pauses millimeters from mine.

"I shouldn't be doing this," he mutters, but he doesn't stop.

Our breath mingles for a moment, his heat searing me before he closes that final gap and takes what he wants.

His mouth plunders mine, his lips brushing back and forth as he devours me. The taste of the meal we just ate lingers on his tongue as he slips through my defenses and into my mouth. I part to give him entry, wanting everything he has to offer, needing to give him everything I have to offer.

Rooster's fingers tangle in my hair before he pulls my head back to deepen the kiss, and I want this and more. Between my legs is tingling with anticipation, with desire and I rub my thighs together to create some friction, hoping to ease the sensations building there.

Then he pulls back, panting. "That was a mistake."

I deflate like a balloon, pain prickling at my chest, and shove him back, so I can duck under his arms and get away from him. Humiliation burns like fire through me.

"Then why did you?"

"Because I can't stop myself, Kitten." He sounds tortured as he says it. "I want you. I want you so fucking much, but you're Gunner's kid. He'll cut my balls off if I touch you."

I roll my eyes. "My dad isn't that terrifying."

His mouth pulls into a grin. "Never said I was scared, just said that's what would happen." Seriousness clouds his face now. "I wish things could go further between us, Carla. You have no idea how much I wish it, but your father is my president. You're his daughter. Ain't right."

And as always it's my father, it's the club standing between me and something I want.

"You want me?" I ask.

"That's never been in question, Kitten."

"Difference between you and me, Rooster, is I'd fight for what I wanted."

I move into the bathroom and shut the door behind me before I sag against it. The tingling between my legs has evaporated, but my heart is still racing.

I peer up at the bathroom ceiling and let out a deep breath as my fingers trail over my swollen lips. The kiss had been perfect. It was everything I dreamed it would be and more. He kissed like a pro, made my knees weak, my heart flutter. How can this be all we'll ever have? It's not right.

There's chemistry between us, there has been from the moment he came into the bar in Temecula, but his fear is holding him back and I don't have time to hold his hand through whatever loyalty issues he has.

I step in the shower and quickly wash myself and my hair before I move out of the cubicle. I make quick work of drying myself and pull on my sleep shorts and tee.

When I step back into the room, Rooster is sitting on the edge of the bed, his hands clasped between his knees. The look on his face nearly breaks me. He looks so dejected, sadness in his eyes.

"Kitten…"

"Don't."

"I want you. That's never been in question."

"But you can't." My words taste sour.

He pushes up from the bed and steps toward me. I resist the urge to step back, to keep that space between us.

I tip my chin up, so I can meet his gaze.

"What are you doing to me?" he questions, his voice sounding wrecked.

"I'm not doing anything," I whisper back, the butterflies in my stomach beating their wings frantically.

"You're making me want things I can't have, Carla. Things I should never be thinking about."

"Then you shouldn't have flirted with me in the first place and put ideas in my head."

He chuckles, his forehead touching mine. "I want you."

"Then have me," I challenge and I expect him to take the bait, but he just kisses my forehead.

"Get some rest, Kitten. Tomorrow is going to be a long day."

I watch as he walks into the bathroom, unsure what to say or do.

ELEVEN

ROOSTER

CARLA IS ACTING like the kiss never happened the next morning. I don't know whether to be grateful or pissed off that I didn't leave her with a lasting impression. Maybe I need to up my game.

It's thoughts like that which got you into this mess in the first place, asshole.

Kissing her was amazing. I don't want to call it a mistake because nothing about it felt wrong, but it is. Going there with my prez's daughter is a whole new low, even by my standards. It could risk my cut, maybe my life, but hell, I can't stop thinking about what I want to do to her. I want her in my bed, I want her in my life, and not just as some passing fling. The more time I spend with her, the more I want her. She's a captivating woman and I'm completely enthralled by her, even if I shouldn't be.

Neither of us are hungry, so we get straight on the road and head for St Louis. The city is about three and a half hours away, maybe four, depending on traffic. I want to hit Indianapolis tonight, but that might be pushing it. We'll see how far we get. Carla was right when she said I'm tired. I'm feeling this journey, although I'm enjoying being on my bike, especially with her behind me. I can feel her thighs hugging mine, and her arms wrapped around my stomach is making my thoughts wander places they shouldn't be.

I try to push that shit out of my head. I don't need to be thinking about anything like this with her sitting behind me, especially not after I shut down any chance we might have had. I know I humiliated her. Hell, I humiliated myself, but that urge to have her, to claim her is an overwhelming itch I just can't scratch. I want her. If I'm being honest with myself, I've wanted her from the moment we left Temecula.

As we come into St Louis, the traffic starts to get busier and I have to lane split to keep moving. The city has a bustling feel to it and the bright blue sky is an inviting sight as we move toward the downtown area. We shouldn't stop now, not if we want to make it to Indianapolis, but I need a break. My stomach is grumbling too, so I guess Carla must be hungry.

I park up the bike and wait for her to climb off it before I kick down the stand and get off too. I secure our helmets to the lock on the bike and then hand her her bag while I sling mine over my shoulder.

We walk a little way, taking in the little stores along the main street, but she stops suddenly. When I walk back to her, she's standing in front of a mini-golf place. I eye her as she says, "Let's go in here."

"We're only stopping to eat and piss," I tell her, hating myself for being a stealer of fun.

She scowls at me. "You said I needed to pull the stick out of my ass. So, let's do that playing mini-golf!"

I stare at her, unsure who the hell this woman is. She surprises me at every turn.

"Carla—"

She snags my hand and her heat sears through me at her

touch. "I know you're worried about whatever danger might be coming, but we need this," she tells me. I should argue the point. Stopping is dangerous, but those eyes fluttering at me are hard to ignore. I relent at the look in her eyes, that pleading look that tells me she needs this more than I do.

"Okay, fine. An hour, then we're back on the road."

She grins and grabs my hand, dragging me inside the building. I've never played mini-golf, or golf for that matter, but I get the hang of it pretty fast. Carla is terrible at it. It takes her forever to complete each hole and a number of misses before she finally gets the ball in the hole.

By the time we reach the fifth level of the course, I'm laughing so hard my sides ache, but so is she. Honestly, this is the most fun I've ever had and it's made all the better by the company.

"I thought you'd be getting better by now," I tell her as I watch her try to sink a shot that should be easy. No surprise, she misses the hole and curses.

I shake my head. I don't know how it's possible to be this bad at something so easy.

"It just misses no matter what I do," she complains.

I move over to her and step up behind her. As soon as my chest is to her back, I feel her stiffen, but she doesn't pull away or attempt to move me from her space. My hands cover hers, taking the mini putter in both of our grasps. Electricity sizzles between us. I should let go of her, but I can't. I don't want to either. Her back pressed up against my chest is giving me ideas I shouldn't be having, but I like her there.

I make a swinging motion with the club, her hands moving with mine. I'm sure she's holding her breath and my own heart rate starts to quicken.

"You just need to work on your swing," I murmur, my mouth close to her ear.

A shiver runs through her and I want to roar in triumph at getting that result from her.

"Finn."

Hearing my real name on her lips makes my cock twitch. No one calls me Finn, but I love the sound of it. It's something that's just ours and I like that too.

I try not to rub against her as I line up the ball with the hole, positioning her body and hands how I need them. Then together we smack the ball up the mini green toward the hole. It goes in and she whoops, turning to hug me. Her arms going around me is like heaven, and my hand goes to the back of her neck, tangling in the hair there. Then our mouths are latched on to each other's.

I don't know who kissed who first. I don't care either. I take everything that she's offering and if we weren't standing in the middle of a mini-golf course I'd take more.

She pulls back breathlessly.

"We have to stop doing that."

I give her a lazy smile. "Why?"

"Because you're making me feel things I don't want to feel."

I tuck a stray piece of hair that has escaped from her braid behind her ear and then I brush my lips back over hers.

"Way to kick a guy in the nuts, Kitten."

Carla peers up at me and I trail my fingers over her tattooed arms.

"I don't mean it like that."

"I know, and you're making me feel things too," I tell her, my voice soft.

"Finn…"

I take her mouth again before she can protest, before she can say any words that can't be taken back and she melts against me.

I could get used to this, but Carla isn't going to stay in

New Jersey forever. Once the danger is passed, she'll return back to her life in Temecula. Thinking about that makes my stomach clench. I don't want her to leave, but I don't want to scare her either, because the only thought rolling through my head right now is that she's mine, and I'm not willing to let her go.

TWELVE

CARLA

SOMEHOW, I convince Rooster we should stay in St Louis and head for Indianapolis tomorrow. He's tired. I can see it in his face. I am too. He isn't happy about it, but he makes a call to my dad to tell him of the delay while I'm settling us into the motel room we rent for the night.

I quickly Google how far it is from St Louis to Jersey and realize we only have fourteen hours of riding time left. That means another two days max on the road. My heart sinks. I'm not sure I'm ready to give up our road trip yet. I'm barely scratching the surface of who Rooster is and beneath that cocky, brazen veneer lies a good man, one I really want to get to know better.

Rooster holds the phone out to me. "Your pop wants to talk to you."

I take the phone and sit up on the bed. "Hey, Dad."

"Hey, sweet girl. How are you doing? I'm sorry this trip is taking so long."

I'm not, so I shrug and say, "It's fine."

"Rooster reckons if you guys ride pretty flat out you can make Jersey in two days."

My heart sinks as he states the information I'm trying to ignore. I don't want to be reminded our tryst will be ending in the next few days. Once we get to the clubhouse, Rooster is probably going to scrape me off. He won't want my father to know there's anything going on between us, and that hurts more than I want to admit. Even though we barely know each other, I feel like I've got into his head in the past few days and he's certainly crawled under my skin. I don't want him to walk away, even though I should. He's a biker. Off limits. He's not someone I should be wanting more with. I'm not even sure he's capable of giving me more. These men are not known for their monogamy.

"Yeah." I sigh. "I can't wait to see you."

"It's been too long. Anything you need ask Rooster for. He'll take care of everything, darlin'."

"Thank you."

"See you in a couple of days, Carla."

I hand the phone back to Rooster once I've said my good-byes and he finishes up the call before hanging up, tossing the handset on the bed and flopping back on it, his arm covering his eyes.

I nibble on my bottom lip as I stare at his perfect jawline.

"Something you want to say, Kitten?" he asks without uncovering his eyes.

"No."

"I can feel your eyes boring into me from here."

I scoff. "They're not boring into you."

He drops his arm and goes up onto his elbows, his eyes meeting mine. I see hunger, need in them. I want to move to him, take what I want, but I'm not sure what he wants. He says he doesn't want to hurt my father, but then he kisses me senseless. I don't know where his head is at.

"I mean, why wouldn't you want me? I'm a vision of perfection."

He's not wrong, but I roll my eyes anyway.

"Modest, too."

I lie back on the bed and switch the television on while he sags back onto the mattress.

"Who has time for modesty? The world would be a much better place if we all just admitted what we want out of life."

"And what do you want out of life, Rooster."

"Finn, baby."

"What?

"You call me Finn, not Rooster."

Heat floods my belly at his words, at his acceptance. Using his real name feels like a triumph. He's given me a part of him that he doesn't give to other people.

Rooster climbs off the bed and stalks toward me, and my heart starts to gallop in my chest. He crawls on top of me, pushing my body back onto the mattress and my chest heaves as his eyes scan my face.

"I want you."

"You have me," I tell him on a breath.

"Your father—"

"Doesn't get a say in this."

His lips quirk into a grin. "I love it when you get feisty, Kitten. It makes me want to kiss you."

"So, kiss me," I demand, between my legs throbbing.

He hesitates for the briefest second and I can see the internal war raging in him before he dips his head and takes my mouth so gently, I want to scream. I need hard and fast from him.

I fist my fingers into his tee and drag him closer, which earns me a low growl from the back of his throat, but he gets the message. When he closes back around my mouth, his movements are sharper, harder and I love it.

His hand moves to my left breast, squeezing it through my clothes until I'm panting.

I sit up so I can pull my tee over my head before he unhooks my bra. He quickly drags his own tee off, grabbing it by the back of the neckline and tugging it in one sexy motion. I think my ovaries obliterate right there.

"I need…" I whimper as his mouth latches onto my nipple and I arch my back off the wall, pushing myself deeper into his mouth. The sensation of his tongue moving over the sensitive nub has me fidgeting as I try to find relief in my aching pussy, but nothing helps.

I decide to take matters into my own hands and shove my jeans down, so I'm lying only in my panties.

Rooster stops, pulling back slightly as his eyes roam over my body. I see the appreciation in his eyes and it makes me squirm more.

"I need you," I pant.

"Need me where?"

"Inside me."

He grins before he pulls down my panties, leaving me completely naked.

I open my thighs to him and he takes the invite, moving between them and latching onto my clit. My back comes off the bed as I fist the sheets, electricity surging between my legs as he flattens his tongue against my slit and licks. He eats me like I'm his favorite meal.

"You taste like heaven," he murmurs before going back between my legs.

I ignore his words, not caring what he has to say, focused only on the sensations pulsing through my pussy. I'm so close to the edge I can see over it and I will my body to step over it as he continues to lave around my clit. Then he pushes one finger then a second into my wet pussy and my body trembles as my orgasm builds.

We shouldn't be doing this, but I couldn't stop now if I

wanted to. I'm too deep in this, too willing, too ready to have him.

I go over the edge, my thighs contracting and my pussy pulsating as it hits. I cry his name as I come, squeezing his fingers inside me.

He doesn't give me a chance to come down. He shoves his jeans down off his hips and frees his cock from his boxer briefs. It's exactly as I imagined—thick, long and veiny. I want it inside me now. He doesn't step straight up, though. He picks up his wallet and pulls a condom from the back of it.

I watch, enthralled as he runs it down the long length of his shaft then gives his cock two pulls. I widen my legs as he steps between them, ready to take him. He meets my eyes and I see the question in them—are you sure?

I nod. Wild horses couldn't stop this from happening right now.

Then without waiting any longer he pushes inside me. There's a slight burn before my pussy accommodates him and then pleasure when he starts to move inside me. I cling to his back, my nails scoring lines down his skin as he moves inside me.

His eyes lock to mine as he pumps his hips back and forth and I feel my stomach dip as he takes what he needs from me.

I come again first, followed by him. His eyes squeeze shut as he spills into the condom.

Finn moves a few more times before he sags onto the bed next to me, both of us sweaty and panting. When he turns his head to look at me, I can't help but smile. He leans into me and kisses my temple.

I can't help but think we've just crossed some line we maybe shouldn't have crossed, but I don't have a single regret. I'm falling for Finn hard, and I don't have a clue what happens when we get to New Jersey.

THIRTEEN

ROOSTER

CARLA LIES AGAINST ME, her tits pressed to my chest. I feel like the luckiest bastard on the planet right now. How the hell did I get this sassy, beautiful woman in my bed? I have no fucking clue, but now that she's there, I don't want her to leave. Screw the consequences. She might be a brother's kid, but I don't care. She means something to me and I want to keep her in my life.

I trail my fingers up the ink on her arm, skimming over the designs that are as beautiful as she is.

"Who did your art?"

"A tattooist in Temecula. He's amazing."

"He?" Jealousy flares, clawing at my gut. The force of it surprises me. I've never been a jealous bastard about any other woman in my life, and believe me, there's been a few.

She rolls her eyes at me before dipping her face back to lean against my chest. "Be careful. Your green-eyed monster is showing."

Damned fucking right it is. This woman is fast becoming my everything.

"I don't like the idea of another man touching you."

She makes a scoffing noise. "You do know I didn't come to bed with you a blushing virgin, right?"

I resist the urge to put my fingers in my ears and whistle. I do not need to know about her previous bedmates.

"If this is your idea of pillow talk, Kitten, it sucks."

Carla runs her fingers over my chest, making my body quiver beneath her touch.

"What happens now?" she asks, and the uncertainty in her voice carves a path through my heart. I don't want her unsure.

"I claim you as my old lady and we ride off into the sunset."

She smacks my chest. "Be serious."

"I am being deadly serious."

Her head lifts and she peers up my body at me, seeking truth in my words. I keep my expression completely serious.

"You're not playing?"

"Baby, I want you. I can't deny that. I won't deny that. Are there obstacles to get around? Yes, but I'm determined to have you, if you want me."

Her eyes go soft. "I want you."

I kiss her temple and pull her closer to me. This right here is bliss and it's the first time in a long time I've felt settled with a woman. I'm not a monk. There have been other women in the past, but I never felt a fraction of what I feel for Carla after a short time. I'm falling for her and hard. I love that sassy mouth of hers, the fact she doesn't let me get away with any shit. I just love her and if I didn't think she'd freak out about the fact, I'd tell her that, but it's too soon to say those words yet.

"I don't want this to end," she tells me something I've been thinking since the start of this road trip.

"Me neither."

"What happens when we get to the clubhouse?"

"What do you want to happen?" I trace circles on her arm as she snuggles deeper against me.

"I don't know."

"You want me, though? You just said so."

"Yes, I want you, but it's not that simple. I live in California. You live in Jersey."

"So move to Jersey. I know your dad would love to have you around again."

She sits up, the sheet falling off her, revealing dusty pink nipples. My mouth starts to water and I resist the urge to lean down and take one in my mouth. I drag my eyes to her face, ignoring the smirk on hers.

"Sorry," I say immediately.

"I don't mind you looking."

"It's hard not to when they're right there, looking delicious."

Carla laughs and shoves me. "Can we get back on topic, please?"

"Sure."

All my feelings flee the moment she starts to worry at her bottom lip. I've never seen Carla anything but collected.

"I can't move back to New Jersey. I left for a reason, Finn."

I lean down and kiss her. "We'll figure it out. For now, let's just enjoy the journey."

"Finn—"

I cover her mouth with my finger. "There will be time to talk about this shit later, baby."

I'm hoping coming home will change her mind, that she'll remember the good things about being back with the club, rather than the bad. The way I feel about her, I would give up my patch and move across the country with her if she didn't come back to Jersey and that should scare me, but it doesn't.

"Do you think things are moving too fast?" she asks.

Things are moving fast, but I'm also sure of my feelings.

"Never felt this way about any other woman, Carla. You make me feel shit I didn't know I was capable of feeling. Yeah, it's fast, but when you know you know."

She leans down and kisses me. "I feel things too."

I flip her onto her back and straddle her hips. She peers up at me with heavy, needy eyes and I give her what she wants. I move back a little so my fingers can slip through her wetness and inside her. She whimpers and arches her back as I move in and out of her heat. She feels so good and I could do this to her all day and night just to see her reaction. Her pleasure feeds my own.

When she comes, she fists the sheets and lets out a beautiful cry that goes straight to my balls. I snag a condom from my wallet on the nightstand and quickly roll it down my shaft before I push inside her. Her walls are still contracting as I enter her, squeezing my cock so tightly this might be over before it gets started if she doesn't stop doing that.

I move slowly, getting her used to me before I pick up my speed. Neither of us lasts long. She goes over the edge again first before I spill into the condom a few moments later, groaning her name as I do.

I move inside her as my cock starts to soften then pull out of her wet heat. She lets out a little whimper as I do, which makes me chuckle.

I kiss the side of her head.

"I need to take care of the condom and clean you up."

Carla nods, but doesn't move. Her chest is flushed and her cheeks rosy. She looks divine. I can't resist going back in for another kiss before I stride into the bathroom to clean up.

FOURTEEN

CARLA

WHEN I WAKE, it takes me a moment to realize why Finn is wrapped around me like a vine. We slept together. Holy shit, we slept together...twice.

The things that man did to me yesterday and last night should be illegal. He is talented when it comes to his tongue and fingers... his cock too.

I can't believe I slept with a biker. So much for keeping my distance, for never going there with any club members. I broke my own rules, but I don't have any regrets. What we did yesterday was nothing short of amazing. I'm a woman who appreciates good sex, and that's exactly what Finn delivered. The man lives up to his name as the cockiest bastard in my dad's club and he has reason to be one. I've never had sex so good. He's amazing in bed, and I think he knows it.

I peer up his body at him and smile. His eyes are closed, his head tipped slightly to the side on the pillow. He looks so adorable asleep. His hair is ruffled from the night before and his breathing is soft and even.

I don't want to wake him, so I pull the blankets back,

careful not to jostle him and as I start to climb out of the bed, he snags my wrist.

"Where are you going, Kitten?" he asks, his voice adorably sleepy.

"I need to pee," I tell him. His eyes are open now, but heavy. He pulls me down for a kiss. His mouth is soft, gentle and I melt against him as he takes it, claiming me, before he releases his hold.

"Now you can go."

I roll my eyes at him. "Bossy ass."

"Get used to it," he tells me.

I head into the bathroom, do my business, and when I emerge, he's sitting up in the bed, the sheet pulled up to his hips. My mouth waters at his bare chest, a few tats covering his otherwise clean skin. The man is delicious.

"See something you like?" he asks, a little smug.

I toss my head and walk over to my bags. "Not really."

"Kitten, don't torment me."

"I wouldn't dream of it," I sass back.

"Get your ass back in this bed. I need you, baby."

My legs move before I can think better of it and I climb on top of him. His fingers go instantly into the back of my hair, tangling in the strands there as he pulls me in for another kiss. I can feel his hardness against me and I love that I can bring this kind of reaction from him.

"We need to get back on the road," he mutters, sounding like he'd rather do anything else but get back out there.

"Can't we just stay in bed for a week?"

I feel his smile against my lips. "I wish, Kitten, but we need to get home."

Home. Could New Jersey be home to me again? I'm not sure. I don't want to think about what happens once this road trip is over. He says he wants me, but will that still hold true once the reality of our situation comes to the forefront?

I try not to think about it.

For now, I'm just going to enjoy being with him and see where this takes us. I don't have the best luck with men. The last guy I fell for was in love with someone else. It wasn't Chance's fault. I should have known better than to pursue a man who was so hung up on his ex he came to town to stalk her, but I couldn't stop myself falling for him. He's an easy guy to love, with that charm and wit. Finn reminds me of him. He has that same cocky demeanor, but there's a hint of danger that lies in him that Chance doesn't have. I know Finn's life isn't roses and rainbows. The club isn't recruiting good ol' boys.

It should turn me off, but if anything, it makes me hotter for Finn. I didn't know I was a thrill-seeker until now.

"Where are we heading to next?" I try not to let my disappointment show, but it must because he grins.

"Indianapolis. It's about four hours away. We'll stop there for lunch and then head on to Pittsburg. That's a six-hour ride, so it's going to be a late night."

I want to ask him what the rush is to get home, but I don't. I'm not sure I want to know what the answer might be, but this will be the longest journey we've done in one day. Is he trying to get rid of me? Did he have his fill and now he's done?

Something must show on my face. He snags my hand.

"Whatever you're thinking, Carla, stop."

"I'm not thinking anything," I lie.

He shakes his head. "I can see those cogs turning in your head, questioning everything. I want you safe. On the road we're exposed. We shouldn't have stayed here as long as we have, but we both needed this rest."

I snort. "Is that what we're calling what we did?"

He smirks. "Baby, you can call it whatever you want as long as it was good for you."

"It was good," I confirm.

His mouth brushes mine before his forehead dips to mine. "I wish we could stay here forever."

I wish that too, but real life is nipping at our heels.

We get on the road and head for Indianapolis. I cling to Finn, my arms wrapped tightly around his back as the bike roars up the highway. It's cooler, so I'm wearing my leather jacket. He's in a hoodie. I can feel the hardness of his belly beneath my fingers, even through his clothes and I wish we were back at that motel room, naked.

I push those thoughts aside. Now isn't the time to be thinking about getting naked with Finn.

We reach Indianapolis around two in the afternoon and stop for something to eat. The city is sprawling and has a homely feel despite its size. I like it immediately, but it's just another stop on a route that is coming toward the finish line. I don't want the journey to end, but I'm looking forward to getting off the back of that damned bike. I swear my ass is never going to look the same and my thighs ache from being in the same position for hours. The only upside is how close it puts me to Finn's back. I like riding behind him, even if I'm hurting. I'd prefer to do it for fun, though, not necessity.

We head into a small restaurant and are seated in the window. As soon as my ass hits the chair, he grabs my hand over the top of the table, making my heart skip a beat as he skims his thumb over the back of my hand.

"What are you ordering, Kitten?"

"I'll have a burger. What about you?"

"Same."

Chatting to him feels easy. Even if there's silence between us it doesn't feel awkward. I'm falling head over heels for him and there's nothing I can do but embrace it. I want him in my life and when we get to Jersey, I have no idea what a relationship between us would look like, but I know I want to try. He fills a hole inside me that I didn't even know was there, and it scares me the depth of feeling I have for him after just a few short days, but when you know, you know. I guess I know.

He lifts my hand to his mouth and kisses my knuckles. "What I'd give to be in a motel with you right now."

Heat pools in my belly. "Yeah? What would you do to me?"

He leans forward on the table and says quietly, "I'd fuck you until you screamed my name."

I swallow hard at the promise in his voice and I realize I want that with him. I want it all. The house, the kids, the white picket fence, and it should scare me to death, but it doesn't. I feel like I'm supposed to be at Finn's side, and nothing is ever going to change that.

FIFTEEN

ROOSTER

WE GET BACK on the road and start the six-hour ride toward Pittsburg. We have to cross two borders—Indiana into Ohio, then Ohio into Pennsylvania. We won't hit Pittsburg until after nine p.m., maybe later and we won't head into the city itself, but stay somewhere on the outskirts. I love my bike, but I want to stop riding and spend time with my woman, and she is mine. I've claimed her and I'll claim her formally when we get back to the clubhouse. She's not pushing me away, which I take as a good sign, even despite the fact I know she's not keen on getting involved with bikers. I know she feels the same heat searing her when we touch that I do. I just hope it's enough to keep us together.

I love the feel of her behind me, but as the sunsets and the temperature drops, I can feel her trembling at my back. Her hands are freezing. I can feel them even through my clothes, ice against my warm belly. Keeping one hand on the handle-bars, I use the other to pull her hands under my jacket, against the heat of my sides. She leans her chin on my shoulder and I hear her yell a "thank you" in my ear. I've never wanted to take care of a woman before, but with her, I want to protect her from everything, even something as small as the cold.

We ride for what feels like forever, the winking head-lamps of cars using the highway blazing into the backs of my eyes until I'm starting to feel heavy-eyed. I'm grateful as hell when we reach the outskirts of the city.

I find a hotel close to the highway, so we can get straight back on it tomorrow without navigating the busy morning traffic, and check into a double room. I don't even bother with the pretense of needing a twin. She's sleeping in my bed next to me. Even so, when we step inside the hotel room, I expect an argument.

"One bed?" The questioning lift of her brow has me chuckling.

"We both know we're going to sleep together, baby." I shift my shoulders. "I didn't see the point of wasting time getting a twin room."

"You're a little presumptuous."

Her haughty tone is fucking adorable.

"I'm right, though, aren't I?"

She doesn't deny it, which has me grinning. She wants me as much as I want her and what she wants is to be in the bed, with me.

"We're not cuddling." She points a finger at my chest, her mouth pulled into a smile as she moves into the room to check out the space.

"Kitten, that's the best part of sharing a bed."

Carla snorts and ducks out of the bathroom before she moves to the bed. I watch, enthralled by her curves, her beauty as she sinks onto the edge of the mattress and lifts a foot to unzip her boots.

She peers up at me. "What are we doing here?"

I drop our bags by the door and straighten.

"I thought that was obvious."

I need to work on my game if she's not sure what we're doing.

"Finn, be serious for a moment." Her eyes flash irritation that doesn't sit right with me.

"I can't. It's not in my DNA."

"I can see that," she says, softening her tone.

She's a contradiction. One moment she seems like she wants to kill me, the next she's soft as putty. I don't know what to do with her.

"Let's order room service and then get some sleep. It's going to be a long day tomorrow."

"It's been a long day every day," she interjects with a wry smile. She's not wrong. This trip has been fun—more than fun, in fact—but it's been hard, too. I'm definitely starting to feel it. I love my bike, but there is a limit to how much time I want to be on it when I have a beautiful woman I could be giving my attention to instead.

I chuckle. "Hopefully, the company has made it a little more bearable."

"I guess."

I scowl at her teasing, which earns me a chuckle, but I love that she feels comfortable enough to give it me back. Most women fawn all over me and try to force things. Carla doesn't do any of that. She's just herself, no apologies, and that's refreshing. It's one of my favorite things about her, in fact.

I order room service while Carla showers. By the time it arrives, my belly is grumbling loudly. We sit together at the small table in the corner of the hotel room and eat, the setting feeling intimate. The longer we sit there the hungrier I get for something that isn't on the menu.

"Stop looking at me like that." She pushes a forkful of food into her mouth.

I can't stop looking at her. Carla is fucking stunning, and

she's mine. I love knowing that.

"Like what?"

"Like you want to devour me whole," she whispers.

I grin. "What makes you think I don't want to do that, Kitten?"

She smiles as she ducks her head. "You're a flirt."

"I only flirt with you, baby."

Her eyes roll, which makes me laugh again.

I lean across the table and capture her mouth, tasting the food she just ate on her tongue. She whimpers against me as I tangle my fingers into her hair, pulling her closer. I could kiss her forever. She has the sweetest mouth and I love touching mine to it.

"What was that for?" Carla demands, a little breathless.

"Do I need a reason?"

"I suppose not."

As soon as we've finished eating, I stack the plates on the tray and leave it outside the door of the room. Then I head into the shower.

When I come out of the bathroom, Carla is already in bed, curled under the covers, the TV on some random movie.

I move around to the other side of the bed and pull the blankets back before sliding under them.

"Come here, Kitten," I order and she moves so she's snuggling into me. I feel like the luckiest son of a bitch on the planet right now.

"Mmm, this feels nice," she sighs out the words.

I stroke her hair out of her face. "Yeah, it does."

"I wish we could stay like this forever."

I wish it too, but the real world is only a five-and-a-half-hour ride away. Tomorrow evening, we'll be in New Jersey. I have no idea what happens then, but the only thing I do know is I'm not giving her up. I'll fight anyone who tries to make me, including her father and my president.

SIXTEEN

CARLA

THE LAST DAY of our journey is shrouded in a heavy sadness. As much as I'm looking forward to sleeping in a bed that isn't in a motel or hotel, I've loved the little bubble Finn and I have been in. I don't want to get back to normal, or at least the club version of normal. There's nothing normal about the Savage Riders.

The thought of this trip ending fills my stomach with lead, makes my heart heavy and my head hurt.

There's a somber mood as the bike roars up the Pennsylvania Turnpike. I cling to Finn like he's my lifeline, like I'm scared to let him go, probably because I am. These last few days have been the best of my life. I don't want things to change, but they're going to. I don't want to lose this connection we have.

As we get closer to New Jersey, Finn's demeanor changes. He's more on edge, his eyes constantly going to the side mirrors of the bike, as if he expects trouble. The real reason for our road trip smacks me in the face, reminding me this wasn't about having fun. There's real danger here and somehow, I forgot that while we were on the road.

I feel myself stiffen in response to his mood. Factories and industry start to come into view, dotting the horizon. We cross the river and familiar sights assault me, sights I haven't seen in years. Things have changed, but stayed the same too. It's the same neighborhoods, different stores on the corners of each street, but the same feel. I watch smoke chug into the air from a tall tower on the horizon and snuggle deeper into Finn's back.

We head into a built-up area filled with businesses and he turns the bike down a side street that I know leads up to the clubhouse. I've taken this road so many times, it's like second nature to me. It feels normal, but weird at the same time.

The Savage Riders' clubhouse is a squat single-story building that sits behind a chain-link fence. The club's insignia of a crowned skull with bike handles coming out of either side of its head hangs over the door and there's a group of men with leather vests called cuts standing near the main entrance.

My eyes go to the rows of bikes parked in front of the building, shiny chrome reflecting the late afternoon sunshine. Finn pulls his motorcycle into the first available space and cuts the engine. I climb off, ignoring the eyes watching me as I do and once my feet are back on solid ground, I tug my helmet off.

Finn kicks down the stand and gets off, removing his own helmet. He secures both to the back of the bike while my eyes move over the clubhouse frontage, my heart starting to beat a little faster in my chest. This is one place I didn't think I'd see again. I had no intention of ever coming back here. Dad tends to come to Temecula to visit me, but after doing that ride across the country, I'm going to make more effort to fly to Jersey. It was a rough few days.

Days that were only made better by the company.

I know my dad loves riding, but it was hard even for

seasoned riders going that far. I can see the toll it's taken on Finn. He looks like he could sleep for a week.

"Carla!" At the sound of my name, I glance up and see Dad moving toward me.

My father looks like me, with the same dark hair, though his has a smattering of salt and pepper in it, and we have the same nose and full mouth. I didn't get much of my mom, who was blonde and tiny, and it is just as well because she didn't stick around very long after I was born. I'm glad I don't remind my father of her.

Dad looks amazing for his age, even with the hint of gut he has that wasn't there last time. Clearly, all that takeout and beer is catching up with him.

He takes me in with a critical eye before he throws his arms around me and pulls me in for a bone-crushing hug that leaves me breathless.

"Missed you, sweetheart."

"I missed you too, Dad." I run my hands over his back, reassured by the solidness of him. Since we got into New Jersey, I've been feeling on edge, something that was made worse by Finn's edginess. I don't know what is going on with the club, but I want to find out.

"Come inside. I'll get you something to eat and drink."

As I go to move, Finn snags my wrist. "Find me when you're finished."

It's not a question but a demand.

I feel my father's eyes boring into the side of my head at his words.

"Finn—"

"Finn?" Dad interrupts. "What the hell is going on here?"

Finn's eyes slide from me to Dad. "She's mine."

"Yours?" my dad growls and I prepare to step between them as his fists clench at his side.

"I'm claiming Carla."

I blink. He's claiming me? In the biker world that's a huge deal. It's stronger than a marriage proposal. Claimed women, or old ladies, are the property of their old man in the eyes of the club. It sounds old fashioned, but it means anything I do reflects on him and it also means I get the protection of the club. I get that anyway, being Gunner's daughter, but this just solidifies it. It also means I'm off limits to any other brothers. The club has a code. Touching another brothers' old lady is a punishable offense. I remember another brother sleeping with an old lady when I was younger. He sported bruises for two weeks after the brothers got to him.

So, Finn claiming me has far-reaching consequences that I'm not sure he's considered. I haven't even thought about were our relationship is going. I live nearly three thousand miles away on the other side of the country. This isn't exactly practical, but my brain also doesn't care about that. I want him and I want him however he comes.

Would I leave my life in Temecula behind?

I peer up at him and my face softens. I'd follow him anywhere. Even so, I bristle at him making all the decisions. He could have talked to me before he dropped this on my father. I would have liked the chance to talk to Dad and prepare him for the fact we're... doing whatever the hell it is we're doing.

"Where you going to talk to me before you made this grand gesture?" I demand, crossing my arms over my chest.

Finn grins, his dimple popping out, which annoys me.

"I might not want to be claimed by you," I add, even though I do. I want it more than I want my next breath.

"Kitten, what did you think we were doing?"

"Having fun."

"And we did have fun, but I didn't go there with a brother's kid for fun. I'm serious about us. I wanted you the moment I laid eyes on you. My life doesn't make fucking sense without you in it."

My heart swells at his words, but my dad snags him by the front of his hoodie and drags him so they're nearly touching noses.

"Asked you to bring my daughter home, not use her for your own pleasure, you little shit."

"Dad—"

He pulls back his fist and before I can stop it slams it into Finn's face. Finn reels back, going back on a foot from the force.

"So, do I have your blessing?" He grins, his teeth covered in blood, and I want to strangle him. Why is he poking the bear?

I step between him and Dad, my hands raising. "Stop it! No more hitting him."

My dad growls under his breath. "I'm going to kill him."

"No one is killing anyone. I'm an adult and I can make my own decisions."

Dad's eyes flash with anger. "I sent him to bring you home, not deflower you."

I snort. "Deflower me? I hate to be the bearer of bad news, but I was deflowered a long time ago."

Both my father and Finn growl at my words.

"Don't talk about other men," Finn snaps at the same time my father mutters, "I don't need to hear that shit."

I roll my eyes. I swear my dad sees me as a little girl, not a grown assed woman.

"I see you're still causing trouble."

I glance up at the voice and see Grim standing off to one side, his arms folded over his broad chest, his mouth tipped up in a smirk. He's short, but wide, and I don't mean fat. The man is all muscle. He's my father's vice president and my godfather. I've known the man my entire life.

I move over to him and I'm pulled into his arms immediately. "It's not me causing trouble," I tell him.

"Darlin', you're the only woman I know that can find trouble in an empty room."

He's right about that, but I don't acknowledge it. He pulls back from the embrace and peers down at me, scanning my face. "You want to fill me in on why your old man punched one of my brother's in the face."

I really don't, so I keep my mouth shut.

"He's claiming Carla," Dad unhelpfully supplies.

Grim takes this in without any emotion. Then his fist lashes out and he catches Finn in the jaw.

SEVENTEEN

ROOSTER

"I SEND you to protect my daughter and you come back talking about claiming her? What the fuck, Rooster?"

Gunner isn't just pissed. He's *pissed*. He looks like he's considering ramming my balls down my throat, and I wouldn't blame him. Carla's his only kid and he's protective of her. That's why I was sent across country to bring her home, although that protection detail didn't include fucking her and then claiming her. I crossed a line, but the thought of being without her fills me with dread like I've never felt, even considering all the things I've done for the club over the years.

"She's mine," I say, readjusting my cut, which I'd put back on the moment I was able to. I feel better with the leather on my back.

"She ain't yours," he growls.

"You looking to get your face rearranged permanently," Grim asks lightly. "Carla ain't just Gunner's daughter, she's part of this club and was part of it before you were. She means something to a lot of us. Using her to get your rocks off ain't happening."

I grit my teeth. "Did I say that was what I'm doing? Told you, Gunner, she's mine. Ain't letting her go."

"Ain't your choice, brother." He snarls over the 'brother'. "Ain't someone you can use and abuse for your own pleasure. She's my damned kid."

"I love her, man."

Gunner's eyes narrow. "You were together, what? Three or four fucking days? You love her after three days?"

I shift my shoulders. "She made an impression."

"Must have been a hell of an impression," Grim mutters.

"I can't explain it, I just know how I feel. I want her and she wants me. Ain't no one going to stand in my way. Not even you, Gunner. You want my cut? You can have it, but ain't walking away from Carla, and nothing you say is going to change my mind."

He leans back in his chair, considering my words and his office suddenly feels smaller than it is, as if the air has been sucked from the room. I feel the weight of his gaze resting heavily on my shoulders.

"You seriously love her?"

"Can't explain it. I just know the moment I laid eyes on her she was it for me. Know you don't want to hear that, Gun, but it's how it is. I love your daughter and I'm going to make her mine. I'd rather do that with your blessing, but either way, I'm doing it."

He eyes me like he's thinking about strangling me, then his eyes slide to Grim, who is leaning against the wall, his legs crossed at the ankles.

"What the hell do you think about this?"

Grim rubs a hand over his face. "I think I ain't never been in love 'til I met my Sophie. Never knew what love was 'til her, but the moment I laid eyes on her, I knew she was the one for me. Can't explain it, Gunner, but this shit does happen."

Gunner's expression is homicidal as he takes me in. "You hurt my daughter and I'll remove your balls."

"This mean I have your blessing?"

I'll claim her without it, but I'd rather have it. Carla loves her father and I don't want her at odds with him over us.

"She love your dumb ass back?"

"I sure as hell hope so."

Gunner scowls at me. "You hurt her and I'll de-ball you." It's not an endorsement, but it's as close as I'm going to get. For now, I'll take it.

"Noted."

I push up from the chair and head out into the corridor, resisting the urge to whoop as I make my way to the common room. There, I find Carla sitting with a few of the old ladies and family members deep in conversation. Her head comes up as soon as I step up to the table.

Her eyes crawl over my face, as if she's cataloging every bruise Gunner and Grim gave me, and I see the dismay in her expression. I don't like that it's there, but I'll deal with that later. I hold a hand out to her to take and she does, letting me pull her to her feet.

I tug her out into the corridor and push her against the wall. Her chest heaves as her questioning gaze meets mine. I don't give her a chance to think. I kiss her until I'm breathless and she's squirming beneath me.

"What was that for?"

"I love you."

She blinks and then between her eyes furrows. "You love me?"

"Yeah, Kitten. Didn't know I could love someone, but what I feel for you surpasses everything I ever dreamed of. You're it for me. I want you, and I hope like fuck you feel the same."

"We barely know each other," she breathes the words.

"Don't change what I feel, what I know you feel too."

"Finn—"

"Deny it if you want, but I've seen the truth in your eyes. I know you want me."

Her eyebrow cocks. "There you go, being all cocky again."

"Ain't cocky if it's the truth. Ain't going to make you say the words back to me, Kitten, but I hope you feel them too."

Carla skims her hand over my chest. "I do, but maybe we should just slow things down a little. Take a breather."

If she needs that space, I'll give it to her, but I'm not going anywhere long term. She's it for me and I'll make her realize it, no matter how long it takes.

EIGHTEEN

CARLA

"DAD—"

"I just don't understand any of this," he interrupts me for the third time in as many seconds.

"You'd understand it better if you let me talk," I mutter, irritation making my words snappy.

I love my father, but he's pig-headed as hell and when he's upset, he can't stop running his mouth.

He sighs. "You love him?"

I soften my eyes as thoughts of Finn surround me. "Yeah."

"Really?"

"Yeah, Dad. You and Grim need to leave him alone. I'm not a little girl anymore. I don't need you to defend my honor. I know what I want and what I need."

He runs a hand through his hair and peers around his office, his brows heavy. "Never thought I'd see the day you'd want to settle down with a biker, kid."

I never thought I'd see it either. A week ago, I would have laughed at the suggestion, but the heart wants what it wants, and my heart wants Finn. I don't know how he ensnared me so quickly, but he did. Everything with him just feels good, right, and I need him like I need my next breath. He's quickly become my world, even if I don't understand it. I've never believed in love at first sight, but the moment he sat at my bar, I knew he was mine, just as I'm his.

"Believe me, this wasn't my plan either. I don't want this lifestyle—no offense," I add, my mouth pulling into a wry smile.

I watch as his eyes narrow. "You know Rooster comes with this lifestyle. Ain't no getting away from that."

"Yeah, I know."

"You asking him to give it up."

My temper flares at that suggestion. "I would never ask him to do anything like that."

"Then, what? You're going to become an old lady? Move back to Jersey? Can't say I don't love the idea of you being home, darlin', but I know how you feel about this shit. You ain't ever going to be happy as the wife of a biker."

"With him, it's different."

His brow cocks in surprise. "You can put it all aside?"

I can, because the payoff is him and now I've had him, I'm not willing to give him up. Not for my dad, not for the club, not for anyone.

"Yes."

His eyes widen a little as he lets out a breath. "You love him."

"Yes," I admit.

"He loves you too, you know?"

A smile graces my lips. "I know."

"He's a good man, but he's not baggage free, sweetheart. No brother is. They join the club because they have that crap dragging behind them and want a safe place to come."

"I know that, Dad."

And I do, but Finn doesn't seem like the other brothers in

the club that I know. He's funny, light. I don't see demons in his eyes like I do when I look into my father's or Grim's.

He sighs. "I hope you know what you're doing."

"I do." I lean forward and press a kiss to his cheek. "Trust me, okay?"

"Sweetheart, the one thing I know for sure is I trust your judgment. Ain't nothing I can say anyway that will stop this."

"Nope."

"Then all I can say is he better treat you right. If he doesn't, I'll kill him."

The serious tone of his voice tells me this isn't an idle threat.

"He will." I wave that off. "Anyway, enough about me and Finn. Do you want to tell me why I had to haul my ass thousands of miles across the country?"

Anger flashes in his eyes, though it's not directed at me. "It's club—"

"You say business and I swear I'll scream," I say, holding up a hand. "You promised you'd explain everything if I came home." My arms raise at my sides. "I'm here, so start explaining."

He peers at me and for a moment I think he's not going to speak, but then he says, "It's complicated."

"So uncomplicate it."

He eyes me and I see the heaviness weighing on his shoulders. "A rival club is after blood. They want our patch. Ain't keen on giving it up to them, so we're butting heads. They made some threats against a couple of the old ladies. I got freaked and sent Rooster to get you. Know you were probably safe in California, but you were too far away for me to protect you if things went wrong. I need you home, sweetheart. I know it probably pissed you off that I disrupted your life, but the thought they could get to you and I wouldn't be there to protect you was driving me crazy."

Cold runs through my body. "Do you think they would come after me?"

"I have no idea. Women and old ladies are supposed to be off limits, but these guys don't seem to follow that code. They followed Maria home after work one night and roughed her up a bit."

Maria is Grim's daughter. I grew up with her, so hearing this makes my stomach twist unpleasantly.

"She's okay," Dad adds at my expression, which I'm sure is filled with terror. "A few bruises, nothing more, but I never want that kind of fear in your life, sweetheart. Not ever."

I understand, even if I don't like the fact I'm here. Growing up, it was just me and Dad—as well as a bunch of uncles who weren't mine by blood—but he's always been protective of me. He wasn't thrilled by my choice to move thousands of miles across the country, but he was always the kind of parent who let me find my own way, and that's what I did. I found my own way. I just never imagined all roads would eventually lead back to New Jersey. I thought I was done with this life, I thought I would be able to have some semblance of normality, without worrying about death, jail or the other plethora of things that can go wrong in this life.

Now, I'm putting myself knee-deep back in that world, but I don't have any regrets. Why? Because as much as I'm Finn's, he's also mine.

"You happy?" Dad surprises me by asking.

I mull over the question for a moment, really thinking about his words. Then I soften my eyes. "Yeah, Dad. I'm happy."

"Then that's all I give a shit about, sweetheart."

I hug him. "Thank you."

"Don't thank me yet. He puts a foot wrong—"

I roll my eyes. "I know, you'll kill him. He's a good man. I know he acts the joker, but there's more to him than that.

96

You might not see it, but he's shown it to me over the past few days."

I leave Dad's office and head toward the common room. When I step inside, I see Finn sitting at the bar with another brother I don't recognize. His face is a mottled purple and black, his eye swollen shut and I feel a pang of guilt that he's hurt because of me.

He pushes off the stool and comes to me. His hands move to my arms as if he has to be touching me. Butterflies flutter against my stomach as he peers down at me, his expression soft.

"Everything go okay with your dad?"

I nod. "He's not thrilled, but he's not ready to shoot you either."

"Winner," he mutters and then dips his head to claim my mouth.

My knees wobble as he kisses me like I'm the reason for him breathing and I have to cling to his biceps when he's done to keep my feet.

"You have to stop kissing me like that," I pant.

He grins. "I'll stop kissing you like that when you stop liking it."

I smile. "You make my legs feel like jello."

He brushes his mouth back over mine. "That just means I'm doing it right, Kitten."

He's an amazing kisser. In fact, everything about him is perfect. I don't know how I lived without him before now.

NINETEEN

ROOSTER

CARLA LOOKS beautiful as she sits next to an old oil drum, the orange flashes from the fire casting shadows over her face. She laughs at something one of the old ladies says, her face soft and relaxed. I like this version of her. It's so different from the highly-strung bar worker I met only a few days earlier. She seems more at ease, more relaxed and considering how much she fought coming here, I'm surprised to see it.

Our road trip changed her, and for the better. Carla is a different person from the one who left Temecula. She seems at ease with everything happening around her and I dare myself to believe a relationship between us could be possible.

Her eyes meet mine and she smiles, which makes my body relax. She puts me at ease in a way I've never felt.

Needing to touch her, to have her near me, I make my way over to her and slip in behind her, pulling her against my chest. She moves willingly and I love the feel of her sitting between my legs. I kiss the top of her head as she pulls my arms around her.

"Happy?" I ask.

She nods. "Yes. Are you?"

"I like having you against me."

"How's your face?"

It hurts, but I'm not telling her that. I don't want her to feel bad for what happened, especially when I deserved it. I should have talked to Gunner, rather than dropping the bombshell on him that I was claiming his kid. He might have been more receptive to me if I had. I know what my brothers think of me—I'm a cocky bastard who doesn't care about other people's feelings. It couldn't be further from the truth, though I am a man who sees what he wants and takes it.

And I want her. I wanted Carla the moment I met her. I love the fact she's sassy and doesn't take my crap. That's the kind of woman I need in my life.

"How did I get so lucky?" she asks.

"Well, I am a good catch," I tell her on a smirk.

I know her eyes are rolling, even though she's not looking at me. "You would think that."

"You don't agree?"

"I think you have a big head that I'm not making any bigger."

"My head is proportional to the rest of my body."

"You're a nut," she tells me and I grin as she leans back against me. I could sit like this forever.

"You want something to eat?" I ask her.

She shakes her head. "I already ate something, but you should get something if you want."

"I'm good, Kitten."

Carla peers up at me and I want to capture her mouth, but she speaks before I can. "Is it weird that I miss being on the road?"

"I miss having you to myself."

"I miss that too," she says softly.

I stroke my hands over her belly as she nuzzles against me. "Love you, baby."

She moves so she can look up at me and her mouth comes to mine. She tastes of the beer she's drinking and a unique taste that is just Carla. I want to devour her whole, sink into her tight pussy, but I'm also aware her father—my president —is somewhere in the grounds of the clubhouse and the last thing I need is another black eye for disrespecting his daughter.

There was a time when I would have just had my fill in front of everyone, not caring who saw my ass naked, but I can't do that to Carla. She's not a club bunny. She's not someone I can just use and discard, as I have done in the past. I'm not proud of the man I was before her, but I won't apologize for it either. I did what I did and I've done a lot of shit in my life I can't take back, but for the first time ever I feel like I'm on the right track.

I want to be a better man for her.

"I love you too," she whispers and her words hit me square in the chest. Hearing them unravels me, makes me feel something I've never felt before in my life.

Whole.

I kiss her, needing to feel her close, needing her and she thankfully gives me all that sweet back. My heart races as she threads her fingers through my hair, pulling me closer.

"I wish we were alone right now," she says with a lazy smile that makes my balls ache. I wish that too. I want to take her, feel her pussy around my cock while I love on her, but that's not going to happen yet. Maybe once we get upstairs. She's sleeping in my bed. She doesn't know it yet, but it's going to happen. I've got used to having her in my arms in bed and I'm not letting go of that just because our road trip is over. I'm not done with her yet.

My phone vibrates in my pocket, breaking the moment

and I shift her slightly so I can pull it out. When I peer at the screen, my heart rate picks up for a different reason. I wriggle out from under Carla, muttering, "I have to take this."

She doesn't seem to notice my change in demeanor, just lets out a sleepy, "Okay."

I move away from the fire and over to the shadows, my stomach filling with ice as I swipe my finger over the screen.

"Janie?"

"I need you to come and look after the kids."

"Why can't you?"

"I'm busy," she snaps. *"You want to be their father—act like it."*

I growl a curse and run a hand over my face. "Fine, I'll be there in ten. Don't fucking leave them alone," I let the threat and between us, then I hang up.

"Fucking hell," I mutter.

I glance at Carla who is falling asleep in front of the barrel before my eyes scan for Gunner. Finding him talking to Grim and Bullet, relief floods me. He'll take care of her. Meanwhile, I need to take care of my kids, who I haven't yet mentioned to Carla. I'm guessing her dad hasn't either, because she hasn't brought it up, but we're way past time for me to come clean about the fact I'm a father who is still technically very married.

Fuck.

TWENTY

CARLA

FINN DOESN'T COME BACK to me and I start to get worried. I push to my feet, pulling my jacket around my body to stave off the cooler night air. As I peer around the grounds of the club, I don't see Finn anywhere. He only stepped away to take a call. He should have been back by now.

I move from fire to fire, trying to see if he's got caught up talking to someone else, but he's nowhere to be seen. Worry starts to gnaw at my gut. Where the hell could he be?

Considering there's danger coming at the club, my first thought is what if something has happened to him? Has someone from the rival club attacked and taken him somewhere?

Fear licks up my spine as I try to find my father. Instead, I run into Marla, Bullet's old lady, a petite red head wearing leather pants and a cropped top.

"You okay there?" she asks as I apologize.

"I'm looking for Finn—Rooster," I correct.

"Haven't seen him for a while."

"He took a call and that's the last I saw of him. I'm worried."

"He'll be around, darlin'. You tried calling him?"

I shake my head and move away from the noise to dial his number. It rings out on the first attempt, so I hang up and try again. This time, the call connects. It's not Finn's voice that answers, though. It's a woman.

"Yeah?"

"I'm uh… looking for Finn."

There's a pause then, *"Who's this?"*

"Carla. Who's this?"

"Janie."

A strange icy feeling erodes at my belly. "Janie?"

"His wife." My stomach contracts painfully as my heart shatters into a million pieces. Shock renders me immobile. He has a wife? Is she serious?

"He's married?" My words shake more than I would like as I whisper this.

"With two boys. You one of those bitches he keeps hooking up with? You know you're wrecking a happy home, right?"

My mouth dries out as her words rattle around my brain. He's married.

"I… what?"

She lets out a huffy breath. *"You didn't know, did you?"*

Her words are a lance to the chest. "I had no idea," I murmur, stumbling back.

The question is why in the hell didn't my father mention the man I'm very much in love with has a whole other family? Does he know?

He's married and has kids? Of course he does. Why did I think I meant anything to him?

"Stay the fuck away from my husband. He's mine, and he'll always be mine. It's me he comes home to, it's me and my boys he takes care of. Stay out of my way, bitch."

The line goes dead and I blink frantically at the screen. I

don't blame her anger, but I don't like having it directed at me.

I stagger toward his room in the clubhouse, my head reeling. I just had the best few days of my life without realizing I was playing a homewrecker. I would never take a man from his wife. Ever. I hate him for putting me in this position. I hate him for making me a person I'm not.

Humiliation burns through me as I push inside the room. I should stay, have this out with him, but I can't. Shame crawls over my skin, covering me in the filth of his lies. I don't care what is going down with the club. I don't care if it's not safe to be out there, staying here is worse. If I stay, I might strangle him with my bare hands.

I grab my bag of belongings and call a cab. Getting out of the clubhouse is surprisingly easy. Everyone is preoccupied with the party, so I slip away unannounced.

I manage to get a last-minute seat on a flight back to California, and as soon as I'm in the air, I text my father and tell him I've left. He messages back immediately, demanding to know what the hell I'm doing, but I switch my phone off and shove it in my bag. I can't talk to him yet. If he knew Finn was married, which he must have done considering he makes it his business to know exactly what is going on with his boys, then he's just as bad as Finn. Running away is probably the childish thing to do, but I did what I always did when things get hard. I leave. It's not the first time I've run, likely it won't be the last, but this time I feel like my heart was left in Jersey.

By the time I get home, I'm exhausted. My apartment feels strange when I step inside it, empty, lonely in a way it never did before I met Finn.

I hate him for that too.

How did I fall for that cocky, good guy routine? What a jackass. I hate him for making me feel for him, for going against my own rules and going there with a biker. I should have known better.

I toss my bag near the front door and make my way to the bathroom. I take a shower, trying to keep my tears at bay, but finally I give into them, letting them fall unchecked. By the time I get out and dried, I feel exhausted. I don't turn my cell on, just climb into bed and let my eyes drift shut.

I wake with gritty eyes and a headache. After sleeping with Finn next to me for the past few days, his absence in the bed leaves me with a heavy heart. I dress and switch on my cell. I have a dozen missed calls from my father, more from Finn and a couple from Grim. I also have a ton of messages. I ignore those too. I don't want to read whatever bullshit excuses he has for me. I've never had someone's wife warn me off their husband. I feel sick to my stomach even thinking she had to do it.

I get up on autopilot, my brain refusing to believe this is happening. I loved him. I still do. I can't believe he'd do this to me. I'm so embarrassed, so humiliated, I can barely lift my head high.

I call Tim, my boss, and tell him I'll make my shift tonight. Then I do everything I can to forget Finn 'Rooster' Reilly ever existed.

TWENTY-ONE

ROOSTER

DEALING with Janie leaves me exhausted. That woman is a nightmare. If it wasn't for the kids, I'd never deal with her ass again. I leave her house, my brain ready to short circuit, and pull out my cell. I sent a message to Carla last night to tell her to head to bed without me, but I didn't hear shit back. That has my senses tingling. Has the bubble we were in finally burst? Has she woken up and realized what a waste of space I am?

Knives stab my gut when I see no messages from her this morning either. Damn, my Kitten can seriously hold a grudge.

I peer back at the house as I dial her number and wait for her to answer and see Joey and Mikey's faces pressed against the window, waving frantically to me. I can't stop from smiling. Those boys are my fucking world. I'd die for them.

Too bad I have to deal with their mother. She's not exactly my favorite person. Every time I try to pull away from her, she threatens to take my boys from me. Last night, she was in the worst mood I've ever seen her in. It took me hours to calm her ass down and get her to stop shrieking at me. What the hell her problem was, I don't know, but with Janie, it could be anything.

Carla doesn't answer, so I hang up, unease prickling along my skin. I also see I have a few missed calls from Prez, so I hit redial.

"Sorry, I was dealing with something last night," I say as soon as the call connects, not giving him chance to speak first.

"Carla's gone."

His words score a path of destruction through me, making my legs wobble a little.

"Gone? What the fuck do you mean she's gone?"

"Back to Temecula. What the hell did you do to her, you little shit? I told you I'd de-ball you if you hurt her."

"I didn't do anything," I protest.

I left her at the party, which was shitty, but did that really warrant going back to California? Carla's many things, but she doesn't have the same flare for dramatics as Janie. This is the type of shit she'd pull, expecting me to chase after her and grovel for forgiveness. I can't see Carla leaving unless something happened, something bad.

"I'll be back in fifteen minutes. You can tell me everything then."

I hang up and pull my helmet on before starting up my bike. Then I tear out of there like I have the devil on my heels. Why the hell would Carla go back to Temecula?

Unless…

Unless she found out I have sons. I meant to tell her, but we haven't exactly been together long enough to share all our personal shit, and I come with some serious amount of baggage.

I make it back to the clubhouse in record timing and head straight for Gunner's office. As soon as I step inside, he looks like he's contemplating thumping me, so I step back out of his reach and hold my hands up.

"Swear I didn't do anything to her."

"I tried to call you a bunch of times last night, asshole." His eyes narrow at me. "Do you wanna explain why I got a text saying my daughter was at the airport, getting a flight back to California?"

"I wish I could, Prez. I have no fucking clue why she'd take off."

"Where the hell where you last night?"

I scrub a hand over my face, tension making my muscles in my shoulders bunch. "Janie called."

I don't say more. He knows what that means. Everyone knows Janie is crazy and that she uses my boys against me whenever she can. I should never have gotten involved with her ass, but now I'm linked to her for years because of my sons.

"Carla know about Janie?"

"We didn't exactly have a conversation about it, Gunner."

"You think she could have found out about your situation?"

I scowl. "How?"

A thought occurs to me and it's not a good one. I pull my phone out and scan through the call log. There's a call from Carla last night, and it lasted three and a half minutes. I never answered any calls from her, so the only person she could have spoken to is Janie.

Fuck.

"Janie must have spoken to her."

Gunner's eyes flare. "You should have told Carla about her. You wouldn't be in this situation right now, and my daughter wouldn't be out there, at risk again. Fuck!"

He slams his hand on the desk and I get his frustration. I

feel it too. She's out there, in danger, because of me, and I hate that.

"You get your ass to Temecula and you bring my daughter back here safely. I don't give a fuck what you have to do to make it happen, you fix this, Rooster. You hear me?"

It's hard not to hear him, considering his voice has raised a full octave and doubled its decibels.

"I'm sorry," I mutter. "Didn't think it would come out like this."

I didn't expect Carla to run when she found out either. She doesn't strike me as the type. I thought she'd be more likely to kick me in the nuts. The fact she has run makes me worry this thing between us might not be fixable.

I push that thought aside. No matter what happens, I'm keeping my promise to Prez, and I'm bringing my woman home, where she belongs.

I head out to my bike, and for the third time, I start the long journey across the country to California.

TWENTY-TWO

CARLA

OVER A FEW DAYS, I settle back into my routine. I try to forget about Rooster and his false promises. My heart is heavy and feels like someone took a knife to it, slicing chunks of it, shredding it to pieces. I was an idiot for falling so hard, so fast, but that connection between us couldn't be denied. It doesn't mean I'm not breaking apart either, because I am. I miss sleeping next to him. I miss his stupid jokes, but he's married and I hate him for that. I have no business getting between him and his family, and I would never have gone there if I'd known the truth.

"It's none of my business, but are you doing okay, Carla?"

I turn and glance at my boss, Tim, who is hovering nearby. I can see the concern etched onto every line of his face, and while I appreciate he cares, I don't need him fussing around me.

"I'm fine," I tell him, moving over to the bar and collecting a few empty glasses.

His brow cocks, but I ignore it. "Don't know what happened, but I know you left and came back different.

Tim is a slight man with dark blond hair that is kept

short. He's the complete opposite to Rooster, who looks wild and has an air of danger about him. I don't think Tim has ever done anything dangerous in his life.

I doubt he's ever seen the back of a motorcycle either.

"You don't seem fine."

I probably don't. I know I've been distracted, which is not like me.

I let out a breath and turn to face him. "I promise I'm okay."

He eyes me for a moment, as if he doesn't believe me, then he nods. "Okay then, but I'm here if you want to talk."

"She said she's fine, asshole."

I snap my head around at Rooster's voice, my eyes bugging out of my head. He's standing at the edge of the bar, his hands tucked into his jeans pocket, his hair ruffled—from his helmet, I'm sure.

"Don't talk to him like that," I hiss at him.

He half-smiles, but I can see it doesn't light up his eyes as it would normally and his dimple barely appears. I move to the end of the bar and he follows. As I step around the end of it, I snag his arm and drag him out of Tim's ear shot.

"Are you crazy? That's my boss!"

His eyes go over my head, and I see fire flare through them. "Don't like the way that fucker was looking at you."

I fold my arms over my chest. The audacity of this man! "Since I'm not yours, I don't see why that matters."

Not that Tim was looking at me in any way but that of a friend.

Rooster's eyes drop to my hair, taking in my tight curls. "Love this look on you, Kitten."

My heart clenches painfully.

"Don't call me that," I say quietly. Hearing the name on his lips almost breaks my composure.

He sighs and rubs a hand over his chin. "I didn't mean to hurt you."

"You're married," I accuse.

I watch the wince cross his face and my gut roils as I realize it's true. "Technically, yes. I want a divorce, but every time I broach it, she threatens to take my kids off me. Don't got a single feeling left for Janie but anger, but I love my damned kids."

I soften at his words. "She can't just stop you seeing your kids."

"There's so much you don't know."

"So, tell me."

His eyes harden. "They ain't mine by blood." Pain ripples across his face. "But they're my sons. I raised both of those boys from birth. Loved them, gave them every-thing they needed. For the past five years, I've been a father. I tried to stay with Janie for them, but she and I were never a good fit. Told her I wanted a divorce when Taylor, my youngest, was two, but that I'd keep doing everything needed for my boys. She dropped the bombshell that she'd fucked someone else, that my kids were this other guys. Gored me in every way imaginable hearing that."

"Oh, Finn." I cover my mouth with my hands. I want to reach out, touch him, but I'm scared to do it. I'm scared of wanting more from him.

"Ain't divorced because of my kids, Kitten, and that's the only fucking reason. Ain't nothing between me and Janie, and there ain't ever going to be again. I hate her for what she's done to me."

"You know for sure they're not your sons? She could be lying to hurt you." I hate this woman. Seeing the pain on Finn's face makes me hate her more.

"Had a test done. They ain't mine, but I'm the only daddy

they've ever known. I can't leave those boys fatherless. I love them both. Nothing changed that."

And yet again, I'm seeing a side to Rooster I didn't expect to see. He's not this shallow manwhore, but a man who puts others before himself.

"You should have told me all this."

"Wasn't exactly time to get into my messy past, Kitten."

"You should have made time as soon as you realized how serious things were getting between us."

"And you shouldn't have run. You didn't give me a chance to explain things. I would have told you everything if I'd known."

"Your ex-wife blindsided me when I called. I wasn't thinking straight."

He reaches out and tucks a piece of hair behind my ear. "I'm sorry, Kitten. More sorry than you'll ever know."

"I know you are." I let out a breath. "It doesn't change the fact you kept it from me, though. You lied."

"I didn't lie."

"Okay, call it a lie of omission, whatever you want to say. You didn't tell me you were still married and that you have kids."

He stares at me a beat and I can see the cogs turning in his brain as he mulls my words over.

"Don't want this to be over, Carla. Ain't ready to let you go."

I'm not sure I'm ready for that either, but I'm not ready to forgive him either. I peer up at him, and I lay it out for him, my heart cracking as I say the words. "You let me love you when you didn't give me the full picture."

"Does it change things? Knowing I have kids, does it stop how you feel about me?" There's a hint of desperation in his voice and I hate that I put it there.

"No. I'm more concerned about the fact you didn't tell

me." I glance over my shoulder at Tim, who is studiously trying to ignore the conversation I'm having.

"I need to get back to work."

As I start to turn, he grabs my wrist. "Ain't walking away from this. Ain't ready for it to be over."

"I know, but it is."

I pull free and he lets me go. Then I turn my back on him, my heart shattering like glass.

TWENTY-THREE

ROOSTER

CARLA'S still mad at me, and I understand why, even if I don't like it. As soon as we started getting cozy together, I should have told her about my boys. There just never seemed to be a good time and on the road it was easy to forget my messy past. In fact, with her everything fades into the background. She makes the dark spots in my life brighter.

I don't want to lose her, but I'm not sure that's my choice any longer and that guts me. I need her like I need my next breath and I feel like I'm suffocating as I think about a life without her in it.

I'm not a man who gives up easily. So, the next night, I head to the bar. She eyes me as soon as I enter, her eyes tracking me as I walk to the stool and slip on to it. I have to make her hear me. I have to make her forgive me.

She looks beautiful tonight, but she looks beautiful all the time. Her dark hair is curled as usual and her shirt fits snug across her tits in a way that should be illegal. Her full lips are painted blood-red and she has on a layer of makeup that accentuates her natural features.

Carla ignores me for a moment, though I see her

sneaking looks in my direction. Finally, realizing she can't avoid me, she moves over to me, her expression a mask of irritation. "What are you doing here?"

"Having a drink. Can I get a Scotch?"

"No."

"Kitten…"

"Didn't we talk about you calling me that?" She huffs. It's adorable.

"We talked. I didn't listen."

She leans over the bar and hisses in my face, "Go home."

"Not without you."

"Finn—"

"Ain't leaving you here. I love you, that ain't changed, but even if I didn't, the Filthy Reapers are still a threat, so if you won't come back to the safety of the clubhouse, I'm camping here until the threat is gone."

She opens her mouth, then closes it again. I watch as she leans over the bar, her tits tantalizingly close. I have to keep my eyes locked on her face to stop from staring at them.

"You need to go back to Jersey."

"Not without you."

Carla stares at me, and for a moment, I think she's considering all the ways she can kill me. She looks as if she's seriously considering it, too. I interlace my fingers on the top of the bar and smile at her.

"Ain't no point without you, Kitten. I know I fucked up, but give me a chance to fix it."

She eyes me, then turns. "I'll get your Scotch."

She moves over to the back of the bar and grabs a bottle from the shelf. I watch as she pours the amber colored liquid into the glass. When Carla steps back up to me, she slides the glass on the bar in front of me. I dig out my wallet and hold out a couple of bills for her. She takes them, but as she does, I snag her wrist. Carla's eyes slide to mine.

"Ain't giving up, Carla. You're mine."

"I'm not," she says quietly, and her words are like a thousand knife wounds to the chest.

"I'll do whatever it takes to prove to you I'm yours."

"You lied to me, and I can't stand liars."

"I didn't really lie, Kitten. I just hadn't got around to telling you about it yet."

"You don't think the fact you're married and have two boys might be something you lead with?"

I study her face, trying to read her emotions, but all I'm getting from her is anger.

"Does it change things that I have kids?"

Carla rolls her eyes. "Of course not."

"So, what's the problem?"

"I don't trust you."

"How can I make you trust me again?"

She lets out a breath. "Honestly, I don't know. I need time to process everything. Give me that?"

I shake my head. "You can have time, but I'm not leaving Temecula. Not with this shit going down with the club."

"You're annoying," she grouses.

I grin. "You already knew that."

"I have to get back to work. If you want to sit there, I can't stop you, but don't get in my way."

"Gotcha. I'll just be over here, enjoying my drink."

She rolls her eyes at me and wanders over to the other end of the bar to serve a patron. I watch her work while I sip on my Scotch. The way she moves entrances me. Everything about her entrances me. She's my perfect woman, and I'm not willing to give her up. She might think we're done, but we're not even close to being done yet. She's mine and I'm going to make her realize that.

All night I sit at the end of the bar, watching her work, keeping an eye out for any trouble. The next night, I'm there too, and the night after that. I can tell my presence is pissing her off, but I can't leave. I won't leave knowing there is danger looming, and I need her to see how serious I am

She's it for me, and I'm not walking away over something so trivial. I love her, and I know she loves me. She just needs to remember that once she stops being angry with me.

We get into a routine of her ignoring me and me sitting watching her work.

On the fifth night, Carla walks over to me, dropping a hand to her hip.

"Are you planning on sitting there all night again?"

"I don't have anywhere else to be."

"You need to leave, Finn. My boss is losing his shit about you camping out there."

"This is a bar. I'm a patron. Not sure what the issue is."

"The issue is you're not here to patronize the bar. You're here like some crazy stalker, watching me every night."

I put a hand to my chest. "Ouch, that was cold, Kitten."

She grits her teeth. "Please, just leave."

"Carla—"

"I told you I need time. This isn't giving me time."

The desperation in her voice makes my stomach roll. I don't want to hurt her or upset her, but I'm not willing to walk away either. What I am willing to do is give her the illusion of space.

Sighing, I push up from the bar. "Fine."

Her brow cocks. "Fine? Just like that you're walking away?"

"Did you want me to argue with you, Kitten?"

Heat rises in her cheeks. "No."

"I can if you want me too."

"No."

I lean over the bar. "I'll never stop fighting for us, but I will give you space, because I can see you need it, but I love you, and that hasn't changed. I want you back in my bed and I'm not going to back down until that happens."

I push up from my seat and head for the exit. I don't go back to the motel I'm staying at, though. I move over to my bike which is parked up on the street outside the bar, and I lean against it. If she thinks I'm leaving her exposed, she's crazy.

Maybe I'm the crazy one. She's right, this is totally stalking territory, but I don't give a shit. I want her back, and I'm going to do whatever it takes to make that happen.

TWENTY-FOUR

CARLA

ROOSTER DOESN'T COME BACK to the bar the next night, which I'm relieved about. I wasn't lying when I said Tim was getting antsy about having a huge biker camped out at the end of his bar night after night. He ordered me to get rid of him because he's scaring the other patrons.

Considering what Rooster told me about his ex holding his kids over his head, I should forgive him and move on, but I'm stuck on the fact he didn't tell me this major part of his life. Truthfully, I'm still smarting over the fact I had to be reamed out by his wife for being a home wrecker, even if she wasn't telling the truth. I'll never come between a man and his family, and there are issues there that I don't want to touch with a ten-foot pole. Janie is crazy, and I don't have the patience to deal with a whacked-out scorned ex-wife.

But his situation isn't his fault either. I can see he's trying to do the right thing, which makes me feel a little guilty for being so hard on him. I really never intended for things to go this far, but now that we're here, I don't know how to go back. I know Rooster is still in town. He follows me to work and sits outside the bar for my entire shift, making sure I'm safe. That does fill me with a warm fuzzy feeling I can't deny. He still cares, even though I did everything I could to push him away. I wonder if he still loves me. I still love him. I've tried to turn those feelings off but I can't.

It's late afternoon and I'm wiping down the bar, my thoughts on Rooster when the doors open. I don't glance up until the patron slides onto the stool in front of the bar. As I do, recognition dawns and my jaw drops open.

Copper-brown hair, a scruffy face and a gorgeous, chiseled jaw smirks back at me. He looks just as handsome as ever, but my stomach doesn't dip as it used to. Now, I feel something different, something less intense. Rooster has ruined me for all other men.

"Carla Babes." His Australian drawl has me grinning. He lifts a hand and gestures. "Hit me up."

I move over to the back of the counter and grab a bottle from the middle shelf. I remember what he drinks. It's hard not to, the man was in my bar nearly every night while he stalked his then ex. Him and Finn have a lot in common.

As I slide the drink in front of him, I notice a wedding band on his finger and rather than feeling a pang of jealousy, I feel a surge of happiness that he got his happily ever after.

"It's good to see you, Chance," I say, meaning every word of it. "How long are you in town for?"

He and Aubrey moved out of Temecula, but I'm not sure where they went. We became friends during his stalking escapades, but he didn't stop by to tell me he was leaving town.

"Just today. Me and Aubrey are doing a whistle-stop tour of all the places we visited on our road trip for our two-year anniversary."

"That's romantic."

He smirks. "Yeah. I got my happily ever after. I hope you found yours."

I stare at him, almost unable to believe he's really here. "My situation is... complicated."

He threads his fingers together on the bar top and says, "Complicated, how?"

"Where's Aubrey?" I deftly change the subject, not wanting to get into my tragic love life.

"She's in the car with Pixy."

"The goat?"

"And our son, CJ."

My heart surges again. "You have a boy."

Chance smirks. "Yeah."

"If he's anything like you then you have your work cut out for you."

"He's exactly like me. The little bugger drives me bonkers, but I love the kid. Never thought I could love anyone as much as Aubrey, but he proved me wrong."

"I'm glad you found that," I tell him, meaning every word of it. He'd been a wreck when he was trying to get her back, and honestly, for a little while I didn't think they would make it. I'm glad they proved me wrong.

"So, why's your situation complicated?" he asks as he takes a swig of his drink.

"He's complicated."

"You know what I learned?"

"What?"

"Life is fucking short, Carla Babes. You have to take what you want, take risks, be willing to step outside your comfort zone. That's the only way to get what you want in life. You like this guy?"

"I love him," I admit.

"Then get your guy. Don't hold back, don't let fear stand in the way."

If only it were that simple.

"He lied to me."

"We all lie when we're scared of losing the most important thing in our lives."

I glare at him. "When did you become so sage?"

"I'm trying it out." He grins.

Sighing, I lean on the bar. "He's married. He can't get divorced because his wife won't let him see the kids—kids that aren't his by blood but that he raised."

Chance listens to my words then says, "So you're mad he has kids or that he's still married."

"I don't care that he has kids. I care that he never told me he was married before…"

"Before you started feeling for him?" he correctly fills in.

"Yeah."

He smiles at me. "I lied to Aubrey. I went to jail and did my time without her by my side. I could have had her, though. I could have avoided a lot of heartache on her part and mine. Don't make shit harder than it has to be."

"You think I should let it go?"

"I think you should do what your heart wants."

My heart wants Finn. I miss him so much.

"Being angry only makes you miserable. Trust me, I know." He knocks his drink back and grins. "I've got to head out. I'm taking Aubrey and CJ out for dinner."

"I'm happy you got your girl," I tell him, meaning every word of it.

"Yeah, me too. Now go and get your guy."

He pushes up from the stool and slides the glass back on to the bar. "See you, Carla Babes."

I watch him leave, my brain filled with colliding thoughts. I do love Finn and I'm miserable without him. Chance is right, being angry serves no purpose. I wipe the bar where Chance was sitting, clean away the glass then I pull out my phone from my apron. I dial Finn's number.

"You okay?" he asks as soon as the call connects.

"Can you come into the bar, please."

"Be there in a second."

"A second? Are you camped outside still?"

"If I answer yes am I likely to get my ass kicked?"

I chuckle. "No."

"Then yes, I'm outside the bar."

"Come inside."

I hang up and wait. A few moments later the doors open and he steps inside the bar. My heart starts to race and my tongue glues itself to the top of my mouth, much like it did the first time I laid eyes on him.

The uncertainty in his gaze as he approaches me guts me. "Kitten?"

"I'm sorry."

His brow unfurrows and I see the relief cross his face. "You don't have anything to be sorry for. I should have told you."

"You should have, but my reaction was over the top. We barely know each other, of course we're going to have aspects of each other's lives we don't know."

He steps into my space and my heart stutters in my chest, my eyes heating as I take him in.

Then his mouth is on mine. I should care that I'm at work, that Tim will fire my ass for inappropriate behavior, but all I can think about is him and me and this moment.

His tongue slides along the slip of my mouth and I open instantly to let him in. His taste explodes in my mouth and I relish it. I've missed him so much. I claw at his back, trying to get closer to him.

He pulls back, separating our mouths, his breath panting out of him as he touches his forehead to mine.

"I love you, Kitten."

"I love you too, Finn."

The doors of the bar open and I'm so distracted by the

man in front of me that I don't see the danger until it's too late. I hear a shriek from one of the other patrons. I turn in time to see the metal of a gun barrel pointed in our direction.

I hear a loud popping sound as Finn drags us to the floor. There's a beat of silence once the popping stops. Then the screaming starts up again.

I wiggle out from under Finn's body, my heart hammering in my chest. The shooter is gone, so my heart starts to slow its frantic beating. As I get free of Finn, I notice he isn't moving off the floor, where he's still lying face down.

"Finn?"

I move to him and as soon as I touch his back, I feel warmth soak into my palm. I glance at it and that's when I see the blood.

"Finn…" I swallow bile and glance around the bar. "Someone call nine-one-one. He's been shot!"

TWENTY-FIVE

ROOSTER

I WAKE to the sound of beeping and the smell of bleach stinging my nostrils. My eyes focus on the white ceiling tiles overhead and the softness of the mattress I'm lying on, thick blankets pulled up to my hips.

I turn my head and that's when I see Carla. She's sitting in the chair at the side of the bed, her hair braided down the side of her head, her feet tucked up underneath her. Her eyes are closed, and I can see the black shadowing beneath them.

I try to move but pain lances through my back. Fuck. I suck air between my teeth and try to control my breathing.

I was shot.

The memories come flooding back. I'd seen the flash of metal and registered immediately what it was. Without thinking, I'd pulled Carla in front of me as pain exploded in my back. It was like nothing I'd ever felt before, white hot agony that rips through my skin.

I remember Carla and I went down in a heap on the floor, and I'd twisted to see the shooter disappearing out of the doors. I just about caught his face and I recognized him. He was a member of the Filthy Reapers—a guy called Half-Pipe.

Fuck.

Did he follow me to Temecula?

Had he been waiting, biding his time? Was his target me or Carla?

My thoughts collide as I try to focus on anything but the pain traveling through my back.

"Finn," she breathes my name and scrambles up from the chair. "You're awake."

"Are we safe?" I bark out.

She frowns at my tone, then nods. "Dad and Bullet are here. They're outside the room."

I grab her hand and squeeze it. "Are you hurt?"

"No, I'm fine." Tears well in her eyes. "You put me down on the ground. You saved my life. Finn, you took a bullet to protect me. I'll never forget that."

I smile despite the pain I'm in. "What do I get for saving your life?"

She hits my bicep. "Be serious for a moment. You could have died."

"But I didn't. I'm still here, breathing and thinking I'm the luckiest bastard on the planet."

"I love you," she tells me.

"I love you too, baby."

"Don't ever get shot again."

"I'll make a note to avoid any shootings in future."

Her lips twitch at my words. "You're incapable of being serious, aren't you? Even with a hole in your back, you're still joking."

"It's who I am, Carla."

"I'm getting that."

She dips low over the bed and presses her lips to mine. "I thought I'd lost you, that you were going to leave me."

The fear in her voice is like an axe to my heart. I shake my head.

"I'm not that easy to get rid of."

"You saved my life."

"You saved mine, so I wasn't letting anything happen to you. Before you, I was living, but that's all I was doing. I was breathing, eating, sleeping, working, but you reminded me there's more to life than that. You reminded me how good it feels to have someone on your team again. I can't ever thank you for that, Carla."

"You don't need to thank me," she whispers. "You have done the same for me. I've always felt like something was missing from my life until I met you. You complete me in a way I didn't know I needed completing. Please, try not to get shot again."

"I have no intention of getting shot ever again, Kitten. That shit hurts."

She rolls her eyes. "Of course it does. Bullets are designed to hurt."

"Don't give me logic." I kiss her again. "I need to talk to your dad and Bullet."

Her expression is stern. "You're in hospital. Club business can wait."

"Please, get them for me," I press, not backing down here. I need to talk to them and I need to do it quickly.

Carla sighs, but she moves to the door and tugs it open. After a moment, Gunner and Bullet step into the room.

"Give us a minute, yeah?"

"Fine." As she reaches for the door, I speak again.

"Don't go far, baby."

I have no idea if it's safe out there or if the Filthy Reapers are still hanging around. What I do know is if anything happens to Carla, I'll tear the world down.

As soon as the door is closed, I glance up at Gunner.

"It was the Reapers."

"We know."

128

"He must have followed me here. Not sure why he didn't attack straight away."

Gunner glances at Bullet and I don't like the look that passes between them.

"What?" I demand.

"The Reapers attacked the clubhouse at the same time that asshole took a potshot at you."

My heart twitches before it starts to gallop in my chest. "Casualties?"

"Grim's in the hospital. Glass in his arm from one of the windows shattering. Everyone else is okay."

"You don't have to worry about the Filthy Reapers anymore," Bullet tells me, fire in his voice. "We paid them a visit after the attack."

Meaning they wiped those fuckers out. It's what we should have done in the first place, the moment they threatened the club, but I understood Gunner and Grim's reluctance to take us into a war we might not win. Attacking the clubhouse and shooting a member had forced their hand. They'd had no choice but to act.

I let myself relax into the pillows. "Thank fuck for that."

"You saved my daughter's life," Gunner tells me.

"She saved mine first."

He holds out a hand and I shake it. "Welcome to the family, son."

I grin. "Can I call you dad?"

"You do and see what happens."

"Can we at least hug?"

"If you want to die."

My grin turns into a smile and I chuckle. "You love me really, Pops."

Bullet smirks as Gunner scowls. "If my kid didn't love you so much, I'd put another damned bullet in you, although what she sees in your ugly mug, I don't know."

Hearing him say those words has my smile growing. Carla loves me. She loves me and I love her, and nothing is going to change that.

"Soon as we get home, I'm officially claiming her. She's mine and that ain't changing."

"You'd better claim her," Gunner grumbles. "I need to know she's going to be taken care of."

"I'll take care of her."

"You should also divorce Janie," Bullet says. "Ain't nothing good going to come from staying with her."

"My boys…"

"We'll get you the best lawyer the club can afford, kid," Gunner tells me.

And this is why I love my club. They're family.

"I love your daughter, Gunner, and you never have to worry about her. I'll love her to my last breath."

"Know that. It's the only reason I'm okay with this shit. I can tell you love her, and you already proved you'll protect her with your life. Couldn't have asked for a better man for her."

Coming from him, that means a lot. Now, I just have to get my woman back to Jersey and get my property patch on her back.

EPILOGUE
CARLA

A year later...

"WHAT THE HELL are you doing up there?" Finn's voice snaps through the silence. I nearly jump a foot and the chair wobbles beneath me. His hands quickly come up to steady my hips and then he's lifting me down.

"Woman, are you crazy? You can't be climbing on chairs when you're pregnant."

I roll my eyes. "I'm barely pregnant."

And I'm not. I only found out we were expecting last night. I did a test in the clubhouse bathroom before the monthly club cookout. Seeing that 'Pregnant' in the window of the test had unlocked something in me I didn't realize needed unlocking.

"I needed the jar off the top shelf."

He reaches up and grabs it, handing it to me.

"Thanks."

After Finn was shot, I knew I couldn't be without him, so I moved back to Jersey. It was a three-day journey, going the same route as we had the first time, but this time in a car with a U-Haul towed behind it.

Moving wasn't as hard as I thought it was going to be. My need to be with Finn made the nearly three-thousand-mile journey easier to handle. After nearly losing him, I never want to be without him again.

Now, we're having a baby together and I can't wait.

"I have to pick up the boys. Can I trust you not to do acrobatics while I'm gone?"

He got joint custody of Joey and Mikey, thanks to the club. In the end they didn't need a lawyer to get involved. They just needed the weight of the club to make Janie see sense. She gave him the divorce too. Finn wanted us to get married as soon as the papers were finalized, but I didn't want to rush into things. I don't need a ring on my finger to prove he's mine. He claimed me in the eyes of the club, and that's as good as married in our world, but if he asked, I'd say yes. I want him in every way imaginable.

"I'll behave," I tell him.

He dips his head and takes my mouth, kissing me like I'm his reason for breathing. I'm sure I am. He's my reason.

"I can't stand the thought of anything happening to you." He rests his forehead against mine and takes a steadying breath. My heart soars. He loves me and he shows me every day how much. I couldn't ask for a better man or a better father for my child.

"Are we telling the boys about the baby tonight?"

"Do you want to? Or do you want to wait?"

"I want to tell them."

Since his two sons have been in our life, I've seen a change in Finn. He's more relaxed, at ease knowing he won't lose access to them. Janie has been great about things really. I'm glad she finally saw sense and calmed her ass down.

He kisses my nose. "Okay, baby." His hand goes to my flat stomach. "I can't wait to meet our kid."

I can't wait for that either. "If we're telling the boys we'll need to tell everyone else."

They're too young to keep secrets.

"Your dad might de-ball me for deflowering his precious girl."

I snort. "We've been living together for twelve months. I'm sure he knows you've deflowered me before now, honey."

"Are you happy?" he asks me.

I nod. "Happier than I thought possible. Are you?"

"I have you, my boys and a new baby on the way. I'm happy, Kitten." He peers down at me. "You complete me."

"You complete me too, Finn Reilly."

He pulls something from his back pocket. I suck air through my teeth when I see it's a ring box. When he opens it, I'm staring at a silver square cut diamond ring. I swallow hard, tears stinging the back of my throat as he gets down on one knee.

"Been trying to find the right time to do this, but I realize the perfect time is any time I make it. I want you to be my wife, Carla. I want you to have my last name. I want you to be mine."

"I'm yours," I say between a sob.

He slips the ring onto my finger and it fits perfectly. I peer down at it, my heart full.

"Be my wife."

I nod even as I struggle to get the words out. "Y-yes."

He gets to his feet and pulls me against his chest, his arms wrapping around my back.

"I love you, Kitten."

"And I love you too."

And I do. He might be a cocky asshole, but he's my cocky

asshole. I never thought I would fall for a brazen biker, but I love Finn and I can't wait to make him my husband.

The End

Want to keep up with all of the new releases in Vi Keeland and Penelope Ward's Cocky Hero Club world? Make sure you sign up for the official Cocky Hero Club newsletter for all the latest on our upcoming books:

https://www.subscribepage.com/CockyHeroClub

Check out other books in the Cocky Hero Club series:
http://www.cockyheroclub.com

GET A FREE BOOK AND EXCLUSIVE CONTENT

Dear Reader,

Thank you so much for taking the time to read my book. One of my favourite parts of writing is connecting with you. From time to time, I send newsletters with the inside scoop on new releases, special offers and other bits of news relating to my books.

When you sign up, you'll get a free book.

Find out more here:

www.jessicaamesauthor.com/newsletter

Jess x

ALSO BY JESSICA AMES

Have you read them all?

In the Untamed Sons MC Series

Ravage

Leaving Rav was the hardest decision I've ever had to make, but I didn't have a choice. Staying and facing my past wasn't an option. I suffered through hell, but I'm stronger than I've ever been, at least I was until my daughter got sick. Now, the only person left who might be able to save her is her father. Only, I have no idea who it is. Ravage, or his brother, Sin.

Download here: https://books2read.com/Ravage-USMC

Nox

Nox is falling for me, but he shouldn't. I have secrets and if he knew the truth he'd drop me in a heartbeat. The problem is I'm falling for him too, but when my past comes out he's going to hate me. Nothing is as it seems. My whole life is a lie. Everything except Nox. Because the truth is Lucy Franklin doesn't really exist.

Download here: https://books2read.com/Nox-USMC

In the Lost Saxons Series

Snared Rider

A decade ago Beth fled Kingsley for one reason and one reason only: Logan Harlow. Sure, the man is a sex on legs biker, but he's also a thief; he stole her heart and broke it. Now, she's back in town and has no choice but to face him.

Download here: https://books2read.com/SnaredRider

Safe Rider

A new life; a new start—that was what Liv needed after escaping her violent marriage. Moving to Kingsley was a chance to show the world she wasn't defeated by her past. No part of that plan involved falling in love with a biker.

Download here: https://books2read.com/SafeRider

Secret Rider

A one-night stand—that was all she was supposed to be. She wasn't supposed to walk into his bar a week later and demand a job. Wade is used to dealing with formidable women but Paige may just be his match. She's fiery, feisty and he wants her, but before they can be together, he needs to learn what she's hiding.

Download here: https://books2read.com/SecretRider

Claimed Rider

(A Lost Saxons Short Story)

Liv survived a nightmare. She may have got her happily ever after, but things are still not perfect in her world. How can she prove to Dean that she's his in every way that matters?

Download here: https://books2read.com/ClaimedRider

Renewed Rider

Beth knows she has to fix things before her family is destroyed and she knows the only way to do that is with Logan at her side. Together, can they renew the bonds of brotherhood and rebuild the club before it's too late?

Download here: https://books2read.com/RenewedRider

Forbidden Rider

The Lost Saxons stole Piper's future. They took her brother from her, put him on a bike and made him one of their own. Hating them was easy—until she met Jem Harlow. He's irritating beyond belief, pushy, charming, attractive, and he knows it. And he won't leave her alone. Worse still, she's falling for his act. There's only one problem: her brother does not want her anywhere near his club friends.

Download here: https://books2read.com/ForbiddenRider

Christmas Rider

(A Lost Saxons Short Story)

Christmas in Kingsley should be a time for celebration, but with a maniac on the loose and a private investigator dogging their steps, things are tense as the festive season gets underway.

Download here: https://books2read.com/ChristmasRider

Flawed Rider

Noah 'Weed' Williams is not a good man. He drinks too much, sleeps around too much, and he doesn't think he's worthy of a meaningful relationship. Meeting Chloe opens his eyes to a world he could have, but he knows she deserves better than him.

Download here: https://books2read.com/FlawedRider

Fallen Rider

Mackenzie is falling for the wrong man. Dane is completely off-limits, but she can't keep her mind off him. Running out on him after a one-night stand, she hoped she could avoid him, but fate has other ideas. When she's sent to his clubhouse for her own protection, she's put front and centre in his world and has no choice but to face up to her feelings for the man.

Download here: https://books2read.com/FallenRider

Sinner's Series

Sinner's Salvation

Some scars don't heal. Chris knows this first hand. As a former soldier, he's seen his share of wars, but the battle over his own guilt is one he can't defeat. After a mission leaves his buddy injured, Chris blames himself. The only light in his life is April. She's spring and summer rolled into one, light to his darkness, and he refuses to give into his urges to find his happily ever after--not until he atones for the sins of his past.

Download here: https://books2read.com/SinnerSalvationSSW

Finding Atonement

Jared 'J-Dog' Michaels lives every day battling demons. For the past few years, he has been raising his son alone and running the local garage with his former Army buddies. As a single dad, his focus has been on his son, but when he meets Nia Walker he can't help but fall for her. She's everything he needs, but he's scared to taint her with his bad luck. When Nia's store is broken into it starts a chain reaction that puts her life in danger. Can Jared save her while finding atonement for his past?

Download here: https://books2read.com/FindingAtonement

Standalone Books

Match Me Perfect

He's a fisherman, she's a marketing manager. He lives on an island, she lives in London. Can online dating really match two people from different worlds?

Download here: https://books2read.com/MatchMePerfect

Pretty Little Deceiver
(Web of Lies Anthology)

I've made a career out of stealing from well-off men. It's easy pickings, too easy. I've accrued more money than I can count over the years, but I'm done. One last job and I can retire. It should be easy, it should be a quick job, but nothing is ever straightforward.

Download here: https://books2read.com/PrettyLittleDeceiver

Stranded Hearts
(Love, Unexpected Collection)

Rhys Hale is a first-class jerk. Everything about him makes Zara's head want to explode. When he comes to her village, intending to put a stonking big development in the middle of it, the gauntlet is thrown down. The last thing she expected was for nature to play dirty and get stuck with him.

Download here: https://books2read.com/StrandedHearts

ABOUT THE AUTHOR

Jessica Ames lives in a small market town in the Midlands, England. She lives with her dog and when she's not writing, she's playing with crochet hooks.

For more updates join her readers group on Facebook:
www.facebook.com/groups/JessicaAmesClubhouse

Subscribe to her newsletter:
www.jessicaamesauthor.com

- facebook.com/JessicaAmesAuthor
- twitter.com/JessicaAmesAuth
- instagram.com/jessicaamesauthor
- goodreads.com/JessicaAmesAuthor
- bookbub.com/profile/jessica-ames

Made in the USA
Monee, IL
12 February 2021